Dead Man's Wood

By

Eloise Keegan

Copyright © 2022 Eloise Keegan

ISBN: 9798835197972

www.publishnation.co.uk

PROLOGUE

Seventeenth-Century England

Ruben Capricornus was staring from the clandestine, earthy shadows of Dead Man's Wood. As he held on to a tree his camouflage was impeccable, but his slender fingers held a length to them that no earthly human could lay claim to. His whole hand, like a giant translucent spider, was gripping the crusty bark of the tree's trunk. His skin, too white and insipid to be of this world, blindingly reflected the tender sunlight of this fledgling morning.

Teasing his hand away slowly, his eyes caught a stream of sunlight that enhanced his devil-like eyes, black horizontal slate in a mist of aqua blue. His stare fell upon the corpse of a young woman lying in the lush undergrowth, the fertile mass of a thriving ecosystem now cradling her dead and statuesque form. It now awaited its fate, to rot back into the earth and become part of Dead Man's Wood forever.

His mask-like face creased into a dry smile and a shimmer of pride and satisfaction smouldered within him. How wonderful. Her long tumbling curtains of flaxen hair draped over her shoulders and motionless cleavage. Her pallid, waxy complexion seemed garish against her healthy hair. Her glassy eyes seemed to stare up at him, unfocused, observing nothing over his shoulder. They were lifeless and glazed, like the eyes of a cold fish on a slab.

Sunlight radiated a creamy glow onto the scene and poached excess moisture from the fertile undergrowth, but it could not thaw death and decomposition. It intensified its inevitable claim, and swarming insect life was now dominating and feeding from her moist and putrid complexion. She was his now forever.

Pulling her heavy corpse into the woods along a woody path, he relished the heady intoxication of his conquest. Pride and elation pulsated through his veins, pushing him further into the twisted terrain. As he moved deeper in, a claustrophobic roof of dense branches denied entry to much of the sunlight, but he knew exactly where he was going. He'd done this so many times before.

Her corpse would never be found. Just like all the others over the centuries, there would be no trace for the earthly world to find evidence of the truth. He had always been of the elusive ether in the woods, and now so was she.

Silence enhanced eerie echoes around the wild domain that was gently waking to the splendour of daybreak. The ground dipped slightly into a trench, and her body churned a groove in the greenery. It sliced through an almost dry stream, covering her with moist mud and debris.

Ruben Capricornus knew she was responsible for her fate; she had done this to herself. He knew the rules of these parts so well. What goes out must come back in a full circle, and he was just playing his part. Well, someone had to, didn't they?

She'd had sinful intent in her heart. She'd had many a chance to change but chosen not to. He had cleansed the world of her dangerous resolve; it was his job, and he had served the area well, had he not?

Pulling her corpse into a clearing, he watched the ground open up into a dense tunnel. He walked towards it, dragging her into the bowels of the earth to be no more. The opening closed quickly, swallowing her whole into its greedy maw. He left her to decompose into the fertile, earthen soup.

Navigating the woods once again, he ignored the wash of pitiful communication from the young woman's spirit, her desperate pleas for mercy that were sluicing around in the ether. He navigated the knotted terrain flawlessly with a wide smile too elated and macabre to be witnessed.

Chapter 1

England, 21st Century

It was a tiny church but its antiquated form held an invisible dominance, a scarred presence sulking against the dying embers of a rustic evening sky. A robust oak tree had selfishly made claim to the sun's rays many years earlier, leaving the medieval structure melancholy below its sprawling shadows.

Cassandra felt a strange pull towards it, as though a mystical mesh were weaving around the church's eaves and cradling dark secrets. It had an intelligence of its own, maybe with something concealed within its underbelly. It seemed to be transmitting centuries-old vile confidences from its stone structure, mysteries never to be divulged in the twenty-first century.

She needed to get home before dark but this was unfamiliar territory. What had started out as a pleasant evening stroll through the village had led her into a confusing maze and she was lost. She could be forgiven because she'd only moved to Whalley Dell a week ago, and she was keen to acquaint herself with the area.

She'd needed a change of location, a new home and a fresh start since her devious fiancé had deceived her. She knew it would take a long time to get back to her normal, confident, trusting self, but today she would not let her past spoil her walk.

Feeling a sudden shiver ripple down her spine, she inhaled a cleansing breath and tasted the tail end of the day's sweet scent. She had learned breathing techniques at her many therapy sessions; even though she had felt a twinge of shame at having to entertain such services, they had helped so much.

The day had offered a pleasantness only an early English summer could. After donning her blue-linen dress, and with a water flask in hand, she had ventured out alone that evening, abandoning her newly purchased home. It was a near-derelict cottage, odd yet sweet, but there were so many repairs and so much unpacking.

She had expected the temperature to be cooling, a refreshing way to end the day, but she was in for a surprise. A wash of heat had ambushed her senses. Walking outside was like walking into an oven, unusual for this time of year. But everything had felt strange lately. As she strolled along, the trees' foliage swayed above her, rhythmically bowing and rustling in a soothing breeze.

Sharing her company with nature, she felt intoxicated. Secretly she gave thanks for its rare blessing. Her mind was fluid and carefree as the sun toasted her fair skin pink and bleached her short blonde hair.

Now she was lost in the grounds of this churchyard. On the day of her arrival, she had given the area a quick once over, but she couldn't remember this church. She definitely *would* have remembered it, so haunting was its presence in the lush countryside.

Intrigued, and proud of herself for finding such a rare treasure, she explored it further. Following an overgrown path that meandered through its grounds, she noticed a wash of silence descending, slowly sucking away her curiosity and replacing it with an unwelcome feeling of dread. Someone was watching her, an elusive presence hiding somewhere in the shadows.

She scanned around but saw nothing but dancing shadows. A heavy, buzzing dizziness started to swim inside her head. Stumbling, she found herself leaning against one of the crooked gravestones as she tried to regain her composure.

Her cheeks were hot in the waning sun; sweat drizzled down her forehead and pasted her hair with its tackiness. The little church seemed so unloved, decrepit and secluded, as though nothing wanted to keep company with it except the plethora of shadows dancing around her. Like her rundown cottage, its scarred, brittle-boned carcass held tight to the present day whilst entertaining the ghosts of centuries past.

Turning around, she scanned the horizon for any sign of life but there was nothing, just a silent, eerie stillness that turned everything moody and surreal. Her only spectator was the church, its many stained-glass windows watching like curious eyes and waiting for her next move.

Her heart was pounding in her chest as she listened to the rustle of the trees. *Breathe Cassandra, just breathe, nice and slow.*

Anxious to get back home, she followed the path through the grounds. She felt too tense and jumpy these days, ever since that bastard had come into her life and changed her. But she had survived and was determined to get back to normal – whatever that was.

Ancient gravestones crowded like crooked teeth in the high-sprouting grass. Nature had taken advantage of their immobility and infected them with swatches of lime-green moss, not dissimilar to blotchy patches of crushed velvet, hiding the time-faded text chiselled into the stone when these poor souls were plunged into the intestines of the earth and laid to rest.

Shadows from the oaks' branches fell over the sunken graves. Shockingly, her mind was being ambushed again. Did she hear a cry coming up from the deep earth, pleading voices of desperation crying 'Help us, help us!'?

How stupid! What is the matter with me? Get a grip. She shivered suddenly as a waft of cold air touched her face. The breeze played a strange melody as it orchestrated a creepy whispering from the trees' twisted fingers.

A rhythmic noise of slow, shuffling footsteps approached from behind, scraping against the ground. 'That's eleventh century, that is,' croaked a voice.

She almost jumped out of her skin and spun around to confront a small tramp-like old man. He swayed, as though standing were a burden, his intoxication quite evident. His lively bright eyes were glazed, as though tiny fish were swimming through them, and his nose resembled a ripe strawberry.

He was standing too close to her and she could smell his unpleasant whiff. He reeked of old empty biscuit tins tainted with an undertone of rotting fruit. Backing away from his glaring eyes, his sweaty face and his toothless grin, she quickly walked away from him through the churchyard.

Following the path, she felt her senses return to normality. She slowed down, hoping to appear relaxed, letting her body language show him that she wasn't scared of him even though she was. His stench followed her, an unwelcome aggravation polluting the sweet fresh air. She heard his hissing laughter and sensed his foul presence trying to hook into her. As she walked further away, it diluted and dissolved into the distance between them.

Then she heard him shout after her, 'Don't go in there. There's ghosts in there!' He gave a hissing laugh.

Nutter, she thought as she quickly made her way out of the graveyard and up another path. She quickened her pace until she was slightly out of breath. Sighing heavily, she felt angry. That she was reacting like a coward was made all the worse by knowing that she was *not* a coward.

Her friends had used to call her feisty, always laughing and trusting. A year ago, she would not have been so spooked by the little man. She'd always had a good sense of humour and befriended everyone she could. She'd only known 'normal' people, until her fiancé. How bloody stupid she'd been. She didn't think it was possible to be taken in by such a deceitful psychopath, convinced that she had a fool proof inner radar that would automatically alert her to weirdos.

Like so many others, she was wrong. But why should she be immune? She felt sad and cheated that she was no longer her old self; she used to be so happy. It repulsed her that she had loved him, wasted her affection and all her intimate moments on an illusion of what she thought he was.

Now her default mode was a deeply suspicion of all men, and she was angry that she felt that way. But with time and the move to this village, she would have a fresh start and a welcome space for healing. That was what she hoped for.

She cringed when she realised the only way home was to retrace her steps. Looking over her shoulder to the church, she was disappointed to see the tramp sitting on one of the horizontal tombstones. His face was turned upwards to the sky, as if drinking in the fading sunset before it was swallowed by the horizon. She didn't want to go near him for fear of being accosted, especially as there was no one else around.

Come on, Cassandra, he's only a little man, she thought. But knowing that he was a stranger, and drunks could be unpredictable, and that any crime he committed towards her would not be witnessed, she decided against it.

4

From a safe distance, the lonely church was watching her with its stained-glass eyes. The crooked gravestones seemed like a blind army protecting it. The oak, like the rest of them, seemed to notice her too, using some hidden, ethereal clairsentience from branches that were dancing in the honey-blushed light. They were like sensory feelers, acknowledging her, a little tribe of silent witnesses. She decided she was not going back in that direction until the tramp had gone.

The air was alive, and a cluster of midges crowded in front of her face. Fanning her arm, she shooed them away, rubbing the itchiness from her nose and hoping she hadn't inhaled any.

Still angry at the tramp for thwarting her attempt to get home before dusk, she moved along a new path. The sun, still hot, was toasting the nape of her neck and irritating her itchy skin. She made haste to lengthen her distance from the church.

The path was made up of tufty yellowed grass and crumbly soil, dehydrated by the unpredictable heat of an English summer. The horizon opened up with pastel, multi-toned meadows on either side of her. Her feet were throbbing with the heat and distance, but she trudged on, letting this unfamiliar path take her somewhere, anywhere, away from the tramp.

The path roped into the distance, seeming to disappear into a dense wood. It was well-trodden, but was it a good idea to continue along it? She knew that she would not get home before sundown but hoped she would come across civilization where she could assess her location and get alternative directions home. *What was I doing? What was I thinking of? Where is this path leading me? This is insane.*

Dust rose around her feet; the earth was dry as bone. She quickened her pace, eager to outrun the approaching dark. Mopping her brow, she continued, hearing nothing but her own laboured breath and the faint drone of bumblebees swimming through the air around her. She watched them dance in the meadows and hedgerows, milking the daylight of its last dredges before darkness stole it away.

She knew the sun's dying embers would soon leave her, plunging her into the sinister wood ahead. She moved hesitantly closer towards its mouth-like void, then she stopped and looked ahead fearfully. She knew she couldn't risk it; she would be

5

swallowed whole into its twisting mass, with no way of finding her route home. She might be trapped all night!

Just as she decided to turn around and go back through the graveyard, she once again heard footsteps behind her.

2

'Hi there!' Cassandra heard a female voice approaching from behind and spun around to see a girl half-running towards her. She had a ropey tumble of long chestnut hair and her feet were pounding the crusty earth, her flat sandals kicking up a flurry of dust. 'You're not going into that wood at this time, are you?' she asked.

It seemed to Cassandra like a warning rather than a question, but she was relieved that this girl was not the grotesque tramp. She gulped uncomfortably to swallow the anxiety that had lodged in her throat.

'I'm Saffron. I live at Green's farm just up over there,' The girl pointed towards the silhouette of a small farmhouse at the edge of a vast pasture; it was almost indecipherable, a dark haze against the sunset.

The skin of her face seemed tight and red, no doubt weathered by the sun and the unforgiving seasons that rural life in England gifted. To Cassandra, she looked like she'd suddenly awoken one day in 1967, turned a wrong corner and ended up in the twenty-first century. She looked like a hippy, with a ruffled, long cotton dress, a neckless of gemstones and a faraway look in her eye.

'Where the heck you going at this time?' she asked again, looking puzzled. She had a spray of orange freckles across her nose and premature wrinkles framed her warm brown eyes. A glittery blue eyeliner made them seem otherworldly. A frosty pink blusher enhanced her sun-blanched glow, and a candyfloss lip gloss glazed her full lips.

Feeling more at ease at seeing someone who seemed half normal and unthreatening, Cassandra laughed. 'Yes, actually. I was going to,' she said. 'I'm trying to get home and I think I'm a bit lost. No, I *am* lost!' I'm looking for civilization. My name's Cassandra.'

Saffron chuckled and looked her up and down. 'God, you are new here! There's no civilization around here for miles. You'll have to go out of the village for that. Are you a tourist? Have you ever been in that wood?'

'No … and no…' Cassandra was taken aback by her sudden inquisition.

'If you're trying to find civilization, you will be disappointed,' Saffron said. 'Nothing is civilized here.' She was smiling now, her deep stare burrowing into Cassandra as though trying to gain some unspoken knowledge from her eyes.

'Don't go in that wood, ever,' she added in a mellow, yet sinister, tone. Her crooked white teeth glistened in the fading light, making her look like a she-wolf.

Cassandra felt an uneasy wash of paralysis crawl over her, as though she had just been caught in a spider's web and was about to be eaten.

'Where you going to, then?' Saffron pressed.

'Whalley Dell.'

'Oh my God, you are lost.' The girl pointed in the opposite direction towards the church where the tramp had been lurking. 'You need to come with me, I'm going the same way. I work as a barmaid at the pub in Whalley Dell, the Green Man – you've probably seen it. Just part time. I'll walk with you. I'm not working tonight, I'm meeting someone.' She sounded excited.

Cassandra thought her a little odd; something about her was peculiar. 'I was going to go that way, but I was trying to get away from a tramp who was following me … a real weirdo. He spooked me talking about ghosts haunting the church.' She pointed into the distance behind her.

'That will be Old Bill, he talks to them all the time. He's harmless enough.' Saffron's voice lowered into a mocking whisper. 'He's always creeping around St Mary's church. Says he sees the dead wandering the graveyard and they talk to him.' She laughed with smug amusement then added, 'Well, it *is* haunted.'

'Is it? How do you know?' asked Cassandra.

'Everywhere is haunted around here – don't you know anything about this place? Anyway, you really don't want to go into that wood now, especially alone. It's bad enough in day time. It's bigger than people think, the trees are very tall and the ground is thick with dense undergrowth You will definitely get lost.'

8

Her voice became more serious. 'Some people think that wolves still prowl its dark recesses. It's not called Dead Man's Wood for nothing – folk have been lost in there for days. If you do get lost, you'll need a miracle to get through to the other side or, worse still, you might never be seen again! That wood is a world all of its own and has its own rules.' Her eyes were wide with warning. 'Anyway, it's private property.' She began chuckling with self-satisfied amusement.

Cassandra knew she'd just been saved from making a terrible mistake – but *wolves*? Did Saffron take her for a fool? She wondered about the wood having its own rules and thought it a strange thing for someone to say. Was Saffron trying to scare her away? And if so, why?

As they walked past the church, Cassandra realised the tramp had gone though she was sure she could still smell him and sense his presence lurking somewhere, watching their every move.

Saffron accompanied her to the main street where her new home was situated in Whalley Dell. They had walked quite quickly but, even so, by the time they arrived dusk had descended and Cassandra had found out quite a lot about the other girl.

Saffron was twenty, four years younger than Cassandra. She lived with her father, her mother having died a few years ago apparently leaving a void so great that he had tried to take his own life.

'He's alright now,' she said, smiling. She had two brothers, Sam and Joe, one older and one slightly younger than her. They all helped run their father's farm. 'You will probably see them around and about. Sam has red hair – yes, he's a proper ginger-minger – and Joe is younger and has normal hair … well, I mean brown hair.'

As she guided Cassandra back to the high street, her silver bangles jangled. Cassandra couldn't help but be amused by the notion that wherever Saffron went, she would be heard before being seen. An image of a cat wearing a collar with a noisy bell, teased her mind. 'I quite like red hair,' she said. 'I think it's quite cute.'

Saffron laughed. 'Yes? But you haven't seen his face!'

Finally, they bade their farewells. Cassandra thanked her companion, relieved she was now only a stone's throw from her new home.

'I'll be working the rest of the week,' Saffron shouted as she strode away. 'Maybe come in the pub one evening. I'll buy you a drink and introduce you to some of the locals.'

Smiling, Cassandra watched her half-run down a narrow side road and disappear around the corner of the pub, her tumbling auburn curls bouncing with life, and her long cotton dress flapping gently with each footstep. The faded sign of the Green Man ale house was swinging gently, squeaking like an old gate into the deserted high street.

Cassandra was relieved that Saffron had not enquired about her reasons for moving to the village because she'd have had to make something up for fear of anyone finding out the truth. They would only find out what she wanted them to know; she didn't want to be seen as pathetic and to be pitied.

She smiled, proud that she was coming to terms with the horrible events of the past. Every day, piece by small piece, she was leaving it behind her. One day she'd be able to look back on it as one of life's many learning curves – albeit a steep one.

3

The evening sky was hazy as she approached her new home. She walked along the stone pavement through the lukewarm darkness until number 6 Meadow Row came into view. It stood on its own, some distance from similar properties further up the road.

Creamy-yellow light shone out from a naked downstairs window, illuminating her way along the path to the front door. That was strange; she couldn't remember leaving the light on.

She made her way carefully along the cracked, stone-flagged garden path. It was overgrown with wild flowers and spikey weeds, now living by their own savage rules. As she approached the front door, thorny claws tried to hinder her. One of them caught on her linen dress, plucking it hard, as though trying to deny her entry.

Oh God, how bloody annoying! She pulled at the thorn with her fingers and it drew blood. The red liquid oozed onto her cotton dress, the stain as dark as ink.

Pushing inside, she realised she hadn't locked the front door. The familiar odour of the two-hundred-year-old cottage filled her nostrils. No doubt it had accommodated countless families over the years, and many men and beasts must have contributed their own unique smell that had soaked into the ancient bones of the place. The lime-and-horsehair bonded stone walls, the coarse rendering, the saturated dampness from many a cruel winter now baked dry, all contributed to the convoluted broth of stench she found herself inhaling. Knowing it would be a while before it smelt like her home, she would have to endure it for now.

The warped wooden floorboards, oak beams and doors moaned at her, creaking at the slightest provocation as though she were an intruder and her presence not welcome. Their mood had been influenced by the punishing elements of an English climate.

She didn't know the last time her new cottage had been occupied – maybe decades – and the spectre of time seemed to be its most recent occupant. Time had not bothered to clean it, or warm the rooms, or decorate, or freshen the interior. Time had gifted it back to Mother Nature long ago and she, in her supreme intelligence, was gently devouring the house that was built by men. Cassandra had rescued the cottage from her just in time before its innards crumbled away.

Now she would turn the tables, excavate any decrepit waste, start afresh and be in charge. Her home would be a palace. Best of all, it would be *her* palace.

She shivered as she noticed a long-legged black spider on the dusty wall and instinctively edged away from it. It stayed put, not moving an inch, and she wondered if it were dead and clinging to the wall from dusty webs.

But that little beast is still alive, she thought. *I know it is! It is too plump and nourished to be dead.* She waited, not wanting to make the first move just in case it pounced. She didn't really mind spiders – she could live with them as long as she didn't have to share a confined space with them – but this one was a whopper. It looked like it had been on steroids! 'When-ever you see a spider in a house, there are thousands more.' She had heard that from someone, maybe from her loopy grandmother.

What a wonderful greeting, she thought, a *spider, a stale stench and a lonely silence. But what did I expect?* She couldn't wait until tomorrow when the builders would start work on the renovations. Whalley Dell would be her fresh start in life; just thinking about it released butterflies in her tummy.

As part of her therapy, she had played with many images in her mind, transporting herself into a wonderful new future. She had browsed the internet to find the best interior makeover styles. It was all about to start tomorrow – though she now had to put up with the state of the cottage while it was being renovated. But she'd already psyched herself up for that.

Shadows danced all around and she suddenly felt alone and vulnerable. She noticed an old, stained mirror on the misshapen wall, powdery dust clinging to its surface. It probably hadn't been moved since it was put there.

Tentatively easing her way slowly from the Sid the Spider, and afraid he might suddenly sprint in her direction, she walked along the hallway. The light from the front room was spilling a wash of yellow from the half-open doorway. It was exactly as she had left it: piles of boxes and bags abandoned in the grotty room, her meagre possessions stacked up, waiting to be released after the room's makeover. Decades-old stained wallpaper draped the uneven elevations; peeled away over time, it revealed multiple layers like discarded dry snake skins, a faint reminder of the cottage's past inhabitants.

What intrigued her most about the house was its crooked staircase in the hallway. Fashioned from oak and neglected by time, it had warped to create an abnormal, undernourished-looking frame, which was now bent and distorted with a hole in the bottom step. The treads were long and narrow and the risers were high, making it look insurmountable, rather like something you'd find in a funhouse at a funfair.

She touched the banister then shook it to see if it was as bad as it looked. It held fast, not moving at all, but seemed to give a groan of annoyance. The moody sound rose up the stairs to echo along the darkened landing above.

Looking up the stairs into the darkness, she was sure she saw a shadow move. Feeling a little nervous, she shouted, 'Hello, is anyone there?'

Suddenly nervous, she realised anyone could have sneaked in off the street. Maybe she'd left the front door ajar. *How, bloody stupid of me!* she thought. *Imagine not locking the door.* She jangled the door keys in her dress pocket and realised she must have locked it! How strange…

The light from the front room spilled into the hallway and she looked for a switch on the wall. She saw it, a tarnished brass socket with a protruding switch. She flicked it on and dim light filled the hallway and pushed aside the darkness up the stairs and on the landing, its antique glow illuminating the creepy, narrow corridor.

Suddenly a knock at the door – three stern raps – pulled her attention from the stairs. Opening the door, she allowed a gentle breeze to drift inside. In front of her was a stranger, a tall man, fiftyish, with short salty-grey hair.

'Hello there. I was just wondering if anyone was in. I tried earlier, but although the lights were on there was no answer. I'm Tom, your neighbour at number four,' he said.

Cassandra could not help but look at him with suspicion. 'Hello… Cassandra,' she managed, slightly unnerved.

'I wanted to introduce myself. I live just up the road with my wife, Jean, so if there is anything you need help with, don't hesitate to ask.' He held out his hand to shake hers.

'That's very nice of you, thank you.' She took his hand; it felt clammy.

She glanced behind her to the stairs, hesitated, then said, 'Actually, there is something. Could you just check upstairs for me for any intruders? I think I may have forgotten to lock the front door when I went out this evening. Would you mind having a look around for me?'

He crossed the threshold slowly, and immediately she smelled stale body odour accompany him into the house. It didn't marry well with the mustiness that was already there.

Silently pausing at the bottom of the stairs, he turned to look at her, then hesitantly ascended the twisted staircase. Each tread moaned. Cassandra followed him until they reached the landing corridor.

'I'll check the rooms,' he said, pushing open one of the bedroom doors. She heard the flick of the light switch then he shouted, 'Nothing in here.' He looked in each room in turn, scrutinising every inch of the three bedrooms and the dishevelled bathroom. 'No, there's nobody here. I'll check the back of the house, if you like.'

'Thank you, I'd be ever so grateful. I'm not sure of my bearings yet. This is supposed to be a fresh start for me, and I feel a little vulnerable.' Had she revealed too much?

Walking into the kitchen, he turned on the light to reveal a misshapen kitchen devoid of any homeliness or intruders. He tried the handle on the back door.

'No, love, nobody in here and your back door is locked. Is there anything else you need? Have you got enough milk, tea and coffee? If not, I can fetch some for you.' He laughed. 'You can't manage without the essentials – well, I couldn't. Me and the wife love our creature comforts!'

'You really are so kind,' she smiled. 'But thank you, no. I have everything I need. You've sorted out the only thing that was bothering me.'

Running his thick fingers over his thin hair, he paused then asked, 'What made you want to move to Whalley Dell?'

Taken aback by his curiosity, she told him nothing of the truth. 'I just fancied a change, that's all.' Her eyes were now restless; she wanted him to leave.

'Well, you've picked a beautiful part of the world to put down roots. If you ever need anything, please call. Oh, and welcome to Whalley Dell, Cassandra. It is Cassandra, isn't it?'

She smiled. 'Yes.'

As he left to walk down the path into the darkness he paused. 'Just remember to lock your front door.' He smiled, then started to walk home, his outline dissolving into the splintered shadows up the road.

She closed the door and locked it behind her. She gave an exhalation of relief as she proceeded along the sparsely illuminated hallway into the kitchen. To her dismay, the bulb had blown again, leaving her in darkness. Fumbling for the torch she'd left on a nearby cupboard, she illuminated the small room. Retrieving a light bulb from her stack, she scraped a dining chair across the stone-flagged floor, stood on it and replaced the blown bulb.

Dim light revealed the room once again. Under the window was an old-fashioned, oblong, white-enamel sink streaked with brown water stains, which seemed to be haemorrhaging dripping water from its tap at five-second intervals. The noise echoed, enhancing her solitude and the pang of loneliness she suddenly felt. There was no fridge, only a row of cupboards circa 1950, uneven and rickety, adorning a roughly plastered wall.

Her rumbling stomach alerted her to the fact that she was longing for a sandwich, though she'd used up all her cheese slices. A stack of cardboard boxes filled a space in the corner of the kitchen and she tore into one, hoping it would contain savoury food – maybe a packet of cheese-and-onion crisps? She was sure she'd packed a six-pack of them. Her disappointment was audible: stacks of bubble-wrapped crockery. In her haste to move, she had not written the contents on some of the boxes.

Tired and thirsty, she filled the kettle and switched it on. At least she knew where the tea bags were, and the open carton of long-life milk and the half-eaten packet of ginger-snap biscuits she'd tucked away on a shelf above the kettle. But she longed for something salty to alleviate her hunger.

15

Discarding the used teabag into the empty sink, she noticed a half-used sliced loaf beside the kettle. Taking a couple of slices, she dragged the dining chair back to the table, sat down and kicked off her shoes.

Slowly she relaxed and surrendered to her solitude. Placing her mug on the table, she massaged her bare feet one at a time. Her legs and body cooled as she lifted her dress high up to her waist. Her legs open slightly, she sighed, and relished the release of trapped heat that had pooled beneath her skirt. Tepid air washed over her bare flesh giving welcome respite, soothing her senses. Things weren't so bad!

But she hadn't realised – how could she? – that she was being watched through the naked kitchen window at the back of the house. Her every move was being observed.

***

Stretching her arms in the air and yawning, she switched off the light and ascended the crooked staircase, accompanied by its squeaky protest. When she walked into the front bedroom, the uneven floorboards moaned slightly too, as though she had awoken them from slumber and provoked their annoyance. But her bed was her own, clean and fresh, although her sheets had probably absorbed some of the odour of the place in the few days that she had been here.

She was willing to rough it for now; she knew that after the renovation work had been completed, it would be a cosy little palace with all the creature comforts she wanted and needed. She could start thinking about working again. Maybe she would regain her creativity as a freelance illustrator or perhaps try a new career.

She pulled the soiled light-switch cord in the bathroom at the back of the house and a dusty lightbulb illuminated the tiny room. There was a chipped white-enamel bath with no shower, a sink, and a stained toilet with a black-plastic seat. The window was missing a pane of glass, allowing a subtle breeze to enter and wash away some of the trapped stench.

Cassandra pulled at the threadbare curtains, shunting them along their rusty metal tracks, though they stubbornly resisted closing all the way. The night was now veiled. She undressed whilst running a shallow, warm bath with her favourite bubble bath from her treasured vanity box. It felt wonderful to wash away all the sticky heat of the day.

She surrendered her mind and body to the strong soapy odour that infused the air. At least the cottage still had hot-and-cold running water. She started to relax as she massaged a little shampoo into her pixie-short hair. It felt strange, but she'd had to sacrifice her long, glossy-blonde tresses. She'd been accustomed to her mid-length hair and felt it was part of her identity, but no longer. He had changed all that and she wanted rid of anything he had touched. Anything that he had held was now tainted and repulsive.

Objects could be discarded and even her skin, which had touched his naked body, would renew itself. But her hair, her hair would always be the same hair that he had caressed as he whispered lies into her ears. The hair that had brushed across him in their most intimate moments had been a sickening reminder of him.

It was so easy to wash now: just a jug or two of water and it was done. Rubbing away the moisture, she felt invigorated, renewed. Her roots would bring forth new hair that had never been tainted by him. Proud of her ability to move forward and discard the pain of past events, she felt she was re-birthing herself as the beautiful, powerful woman she had always known she was. She felt as if she were almost there.

***

Ruben Capricornus, a youthful, slender, beast of a man, was still staring at the rear of her cottage. He was annoyed that the light had gone out downstairs, leaving the back kitchen an inky black. About to skulk away, he saw the window above it illuminate. Stopping and peering closer as he held on to the rear garden fence with his long fingers, he strained forward to get a better look and watched her perfect outline move towards the window.

Seeing her there for a fleeting moment was not enough. He wanted more, but she closed the curtains and burst his sick bubble of voyeurism. Then he felt elated; here was another witch in the village to court! Smiling, his wide, impish lips creased into his high cheekbones, and his flawless white skin was illuminated in the moonlight like a ghostly apparition. He lingered for a

17

while, relishing a desire to seduce her. Could he? Should he? Did she have a sinful heart?

He would linger a while before returning home to melt once again into the earthy and fibrous innards of Dead Man's Wood.

**

That night, as Cassandra curled up in bed, her short damp hair a cooling balm against the heat, she drifted into a quiet place in her mind – until she heard a creaking noise. Something was on the landing outside her bedroom door.

Her mind was instantly wrenched from sleep and catapulted into alert comprehension. Something was on the landing. An intruder? She held her breath and listened, her senses investigating the silence for anything untoward.

Sitting up, she flicked on the bedside lamp. A haze of weak light tried to illuminate the room but failed miserably; the eco-bulb could only bruise the dark shadows all around. Although her bedroom door was half open, she couldn't see anything but blackness beyond.

She listened for another sound but none came. Her eyes wide and alert, she decided to leave the light on for company in the clutches of night. Feeling like a five-year-old child in need of a night light, she tried to relax and forced herself to smile. *Nobody there.*

That was when she heard it. She was turning over and snuggling into the pillow when a blast of cold air rushed inside her ear and a voice shouted, 'Get out!'

The voice was sharp but echoey, like someone shouting down a windy tunnel from far away. Cassandra immediately sat up, expecting to see someone, but nobody was there.

She ran across the wooden floor and onto the pitch-black landing, her hand feeling along the wall for the light switch. Panic animated her as she spun round to confront the threshold of her bedroom. 'Who's there?' she shouted.

The ceiling light illuminated the landing, but her time-stained bedroom revealed nothing but emptiness and silence. Terrified, she rubbed at her ear where the voice had communicated with her. Its icy blast against her face was fading now. Hesitantly, she moved back into the bedroom, alert to any slight noise.

Pulling the bedroom curtains back on their tarnished metal tracks, she looked down into the street below hoping to see someone who could help her. There was nothing but a beautiful English night in May, the moon sleeping in its dusky sky. The ripe foliage on the bobbing branches of the trees was casting dancing shadows across an empty high street.

Leaving on all the lights, she tried to sleep.

4

After leaving Cassandra to make her way home, Saffron entered the Green Man pub and looked around for her friends. She was meeting them for a relaxing evening but, unbeknown to anyone else, she wanted an encounter with Fenton Brooks. She had held a torch for him for as long as she could remember; as she had grown from childhood to adolescence then to womanhood, she had wanted him more and more.

There was an exaggerated smile on her face as she looked around for him, but she sighed inside when she realised he was not there yet. A few older blokes were propping up the bar talking to Frank, the landlord of the Green Man. His thirty plus years of service to the community of Whalley Dell, no doubt appreciated by his many regulars, had kept their bellies full of ale.

Heat from the day made Saffron's face perspire and she felt her longing to see Fenton increase. Her female friends shouted and gestured for her to join them and she did. After a happy reunion, she went to the bar to get a large glass of red wine.

She didn't have a date with Fenton but she just knew he would be there tonight. Maybe she would talk to him; perhaps things could get warmer between them and they would become an item, if she played her cards right. Things had not been progressing as well as she wanted, and she wondered if there was anyone else on the scene.

As she picked up her glass from the bar, he walked in. She felt herself blush with excitement. He casually acknowledged her with a 'Hi, Saff', then walked on without stopping. He joined some mates at the back of the pub and seamlessly melted into their conversation.

What were they talking about? She felt herself pulsate with anticipation of her next move. She decided to sit at a small table within listening distance. Her two friends joined her, smiling as they sat down.

Saffron was now eavesdropping on the men's conversation. They were talking about someone, and mischievous laughter filtered through the air as their banter increased. Then she heard, 'Yes, I've seen her. She's not bad.'

Then another voice: 'Where's she from?'

Then another: 'I don't know, but she's fit.'

Then Fenton's voice: 'Yeah! she's nice... I would anytime.'

Then another: 'You would what?'

Suddenly a roar of laughter filled the pub, accentuated by the low-beamed ceiling, and thick walls of the sixteenth-century ale house. Its vibration jarred the air around Saffron. Her ears were seared by the shrill blast of laughter, and also with the realisation of who they were talking about. Her stomach turned upside down with repulsion. She had been chatting with her not ten minutes ago and had helped her get home – Cassandra! The new bitch in town.

Saffron ignored her friends' upbeat conversation and stared ahead, hollow-eyed, as she realised that Cassandra was a big fat fly in the ointment.

5

The next morning brought the promise of another hot day, with wispy air-brushed clouds that would burn away into the deep pastel-blue sky well before noon. Despite the scary incident last night, Cassandra was excited. The builders were starting work on her house and she expected them early – 8am, they had said.

Their transit van pulled up outside ten minutes early, a good sign. Mark, the builder, was a heavy-set bloke. He had brought his labourer with him, a tall, skinny, almost bendy lad called Craig.

After showing them the kettle and leaving packs of ginger snaps and chocolate digestives on the side, Cassandra ventured out for a walk. She hoped the quaint café along the high street would be open for breakfast.

Walking along the sun-washed street, she passed many small shops, some with misshapen elevations and tiny doors and windows. Fresh paint and a new window or two could not disguise their many centuries of age. The lazy drone of traffic moved along the high street, slow and fragmented.

The Tea Shop was at the end of the road. It had a pink, double-fronted façade, and a simple sign. She passed shops filled with antiques and a high-end designer-clothes shop. A slightly smaller shop across the road was filled with crystals, books, candles and other mystical wares. Its window display stood out from the rest with an intriguing, welcoming energy, its bright sparkling colours creating an aura of benevolence.

She crossed the road to get a closer look and stood outside, drinking in the wonderful window display. The shop sign, *MAGIC THINGS*, scrolled in iridescent blue, declared its presence proudly on the street.

Cassandra was mesmerized by its abundance of the peculiar and supernatural. Feeling a curious desire to go in, she moved closer and was ambushed by the intoxicating scent of sweetness and musk. It made her feel warm and fuzzy – happy.

Once inside, her senses were overwhelmed by the wealth of produce: an array of gorgeous fragrances from a colourful display of aromatherapy candles, soaps and essential oils; glossy crystals of all shapes, sizes and colours; books, tarot card decks and angel cards; mystical jewellery; symbols of all faiths. The sweet yet sultry aroma of ylang-ylang prevailed, steaming out from an atomizing diffuser on the counter. A soothing, almost hypnotic tune was playing, its whispery tones chiming with an undertone of drum noises, excavating a mood of otherworldliness.

The shop was getting busy now, as it always did in the holiday season. Customers wandered around, mesmerized by the abundance of mystical produce. Sabina, the owner, a slender lady with long, burgundy hair and a subtle cleavage, was behind the till with her daughter, Charity, a pretty teenage girl with vibrant blue eyes.

Cassandra, not used to her newly cropped hair, felt a little tomboyish. She was wearing a calf-length dress and her blonde hair, now sun bleached to an ashy hue, framed her heart-shaped face. A whisper of blusher on her cheeks and a stroke of buff-coloured eyeshadow complemented her features.

Something caught Cassandra's eye: a sign on the wall in bright blue against a yellow background: *FORTUNE TELLING AVAILABLE FOR THIRTY MINUTES.* Feeling a rush of excitement, she approached the two women behind the counter, who both smiled at her.

Sabina moved from behind the counter, a long silver chain with a turquoise blue crystal dangling heavily against her chest. Before Cassandra could speak, she said, 'You want a reading, don't you?'

Cassandra laughed. 'Yes, I do. How did you know?'

All three of them laughed as Sabina said, 'I am the fortune teller!' Her wide green eyes were reassuring. Looking at her watch, she said, 'Give me about half an hour. Is that okay?'

Cassandra beamed. 'That's great. It will give me time to get breakfast across the road. I'll see you then – oh, and thank you.'

She left the otherworldly ambiance of Magic Things and strolled across to The Tea Shop where a new aroma greeted her: warm toasted bread, coffee and English breakfasts. Taking one of the shaded tables on the pavement, she enjoyed a pot of tea, croissants and marmalade whilst watching the comings and goings of customers investigating Magic Things across the road. She felt an excited curiosity; she'd never had a reading done before.

The morning temperature was rising. After half an hour, her appetite satisfied and feeling energized, she strolled across to keep her appointment with Sabina. She was tingling with anticipation.

'Charity, hold the fort for twenty minutes, will you, love?' Sabina instructed her daughter as Cassandra entered the shop together with a gust of warm air. Its hot breath seemed to infuse the sweet aromas in the shop with greater depth and potency. Hanging windchimes teased the air with tinkling notes to accompany the ethereal background music; it was a butterfly-kissed interior.

Cassandra paid Charity, then followed Sabina into the back room of the shop and closed the door behind her. Sabina gestured for her to sit down at a small table. Sunlight was trying to break through the yellow shuttered window, enhancing the room's mood of otherworldliness.

As Sabina lit a tall, white candle, Cassandra told her she had just bought the derelict cottage at the bottom of the road: 6, Meadow Row.

Sabina gasped and put her hand over her mouth. 'I heard that the place had been sold but I thought a builder would have taken it on, what with the state of the place. I take it you haven't moved in yet?'

Cassandra replied almost apologetically, though she didn't know why. 'I'm roughing it until the remedial work gets done.' Hunching her shoulders, she said, 'I know it might sound crazy, but I can put up with it while it's being renovated. Besides, it's summer. I couldn't do it in winter – I'd freeze.'

'Yes, I'm sure you would. The winters here are very bad. Please don't give me any more information about yourself because it will spoil the reading.' Sabina looked closely at Cassandra and whispered, 'Wow! You have the most beautiful eyes I've ever seen.'

Cassandra had often been complemented on her brown, gold-flecked eyes and felt no embarrassment. Then Sabina added calmly, 'I must tell you that I will relay whatever I get from spirit

24

to you. No sugar coating or fake silliness. I say what I am given. Are you ready to accept this? If not, tell me now and we can stop.'

Cassandra felt a rush of excitement. 'Yes, I'm ready.'

Sabina closed her green eyes and centred herself. Inhaling deeply, her chest rose and fell with each breath. Lifting the black-silk wrapped tarot cards, she placed them in the middle of the table. Muffled conversation and noises from the shop penetrated the closed door and contrasted with the stillness in the room. A crystal ball glinted in the dancing candlelight and Cassandra was intrigued, almost hypnotized, by its pointed flame.

Sabina shuffled the cards and slapped them together rhythmically, their harsh clatter slicing through the silence. Cassandra watched her dexterity with awe and was surprised that her long, pink-painted fingernails did not hinder her.

Suddenly Sabina stopped, as though a trance had taken hold of her. She placed the cards back on the table and said, 'You do not live alone. I have a woman here who seems very angry at you having stolen her house from her.'

Cassandra gasped. 'No, that's not right. I bought the house from an estate agent and paid a decent price for it, despite all the work that needed to be done. I don't understand.'

'No. You have moved into her house and she wants you out,' said Sabina.

'But that doesn't make any sense. The house was empty. The agent didn't reveal any personal details of who was selling it, but I understood it had been empty for a long time.'

'I have a spiteful, hateful person here!' said Sabina, her eyes closed, her head to one side. 'You do not get along very well with this person. It is a female energy, and she's shouting at you to go … to get out. She's not telling me her name – she thinks she's above that. She says she will not be messed with.'

Suddenly Sabina's head fell forward and she came out of her trance. Her eyes were unfocused, her skin clammy, her body swaying.

Shocked, Cassandra gulped a sharp breath into her lungs. The raw memory of last night thrust into her mind as she remembered that icy voice in her ear telling her to 'get out', but she had put that down to stress and exhaustion. Should she mention it? She

25

blurted, 'OMG, I can't believe that. I was trying to sleep last night when a blast of cold air rushed inside my ear together with a horrible voice. It told me to get out, and I was terrified for quite some time. Do you think the cottage may be haunted?'

Composing herself, Sabina spoke quietly. 'Maybe it is a spirit that has not moved on. Sometimes when people pass over, they ignore the bright light to heaven and choose not to accept that they are dead and do not have a body anymore. They can get attached to their home on earth and refuse to move out, especially if they had a stubborn personality in life. They shun the light when it comes to take them, and they choose to ignore their guardian angels and past loved ones who come to accompany them to heaven to continue their soul journey into the next life.'

A heavy mood dominated the room and Cassandra felt engulfed by its suffocating stillness. Not a sound could be heard from the shop out front, as though they were suddenly trapped in another dimension.

Sabina said, 'Sometimes they get stuck on the astral plane, the dimension we automatically bypass when we die. Most souls are guided by the light to the life beyond. She's probably stuck and needs help to move on.'

'Astral plane?' quizzed Cassandra.

'It is a crowded realm of the tormented dead, where souls reside when they ignore the welcoming light of their angels or spirit guides. They refuse to accept that they are dead for whatever reason and try to get back to their lives on earth, but they cannot because they have no body to return to. They often had a very bitter personality in life and unfortunately their temperament holds them back. The majority of us accept the light that frees us, but they do not.'

Reassuringly, she continued, 'There is help available, so please don't worry. It also benefits the trapped soul, who can be moved on into the lighter dimensions where they belong. Sometimes it needs specialist help, but usually it can be dealt with easily enough if you know what you're doing. Just let me know if it persists.'

'I'm scared now that I have a ghost in my new home,' said Cassandra.

Sabina laughed. 'It can't hurt you, Cassandra, although it may be a little annoying at times. I have moved many an earth-bound spirit out of a house. Usually, they are trapped through a fear of moving on.' She smiled reassuringly and lowered her eyes to the deck of tarot cards. The dancing flame of the candle stretched high between them.

Using her pincer-like fingernails, Sabina pulled out three cards and laid them face down on the table. The first one she turned over was The Tower XVI, a colourful card depicting two unfortunate souls falling from a fire-struck medieval structure. A lightning bolt had ruptured its roof.

Cassandra waited for Sabina to speak. She wasn't sceptical anymore and wondered what the woman would say next.

'This is your past. I feel you have had a tower moment in your life where all your plans and dreams fell apart. It's not dissimilar to having the rug pulled from under your feet.'

Cassandra felt a chill run down her spine.

Sabina went on. 'Your heart was broken, not just by one person but by the deceit of someone close – maybe a family member?'

Cassandra stayed silent but was moved by her accuracy. She longed to find out more but was afraid that Sabina would reveal something she wanted to keep secret.

'It feels like a terrible betrayal. Something unforgivable was done to you, and you couldn't get your head around it. Sadly, those people are no longer in your life. It feels as though it totally destroyed you for a while.'

Knowing how accurate the interpretation was, Cassandra felt her heart beat faster.

Sabina closed her eyes and went into a trance-like state again. There was a heavy sensation in the room and Cassandra felt a tingling energy around her; she could almost see and touch it. The hairs on her arms bristled as a swirling vortex surrounded them.

Sabina's voice rose. 'I see a church, a ceremony, a wedding with no groom. I see a wedding cake with a bride on top but the groom is falling down, down. I see much cruelty, deceit and pain. I see a traitor skulking away in the shadows.'

She slowly came out of her trance. She opened her eyes and met Cassandra's stunned stare; two pools of earthy green staring into two pools of hazel brown.

She reached out and took Cassandra's hands. 'My poor love, your wedding did not happen, did it? Such an awful deceit – but you are moving on now.'

Cassandra stood up and her wooden chair scraped against the stone-flagged floor. Feeling humiliated and betrayed all over again, she stared at Sabina with tear-filled eyes. 'Who, told you? Someone told you, didn't they? You can't have known. Well, not like that!'

Like a video screen in her mind, Cassandra re-lived the betrayal and felt the familiar pain slash at her insides from her bowels up to her throat. It played out perfectly in sequence, not stopping until it was complete. Her mind could not cope. She looked for an explanation, a why, as though the situation could be changed. It could not.

Sabina was uncomfortable, too. She stood up and reached out her hand. 'Cassandra, sometimes the words just come out and I have no control over them.' She spoke quietly. 'I let the spirit guide me. You have my strictest confidence that nothing goes beyond these four walls. Your message is for you and only you. Please, you can trust me!'

They both sat down again. Although Cassandra was upset and shocked, she was also impressed by Sabina's accuracy. Wiping away her tears, she let her continue the reading.

Sabina concentrated and turned over the next card. It was The Emperor IV, showing a middle-aged man sitting on a throne holding a sceptre and cross, with a phoenix at his feet. Relieved, her smile widened. 'This is a card of stability and victory. Your home will become your haven, and you will be protected by wise authority. You will finally be in charge of your own life and your plans will come to fruition. The divine is on your side, watching over you. You will develop a friendship with a man, a kind man who will steer you to happiness.'

The trance fell upon her again. 'I see much beauty. I see a meadow with butterflies swimming in the air... I see a castle upon a hill shimmering with gold leaf in the sunshine. I see clouds.'

She suddenly stopped and her breathing grew faster, indicating to Cassandra that now she was seeing something disturbing that she didn't want to share. Wide-eyed, she stopped abruptly. 'I'm sorry Cassandra, I don't know what happened then. Spirit couldn't quite get through.'

Cassandra wondered what she had seen in her vision and hoped it wasn't anything bad. She instinctively knew Sabina was withholding something she was afraid to share.

Sabina revealed the last card, The Moon XVIII, and silence dominated as they looked at its images. It displayed angry dogs barking and snarling at a face in the moon, as though they were being provoked and tormented by its energy. A fiery-red lobster wading in a pool of water enhanced the mystery of the message.

Sabina focused on the card with her intense green eyes, her breathing audible. Trying to compose herself, she said, 'I see a woman again, but she is younger and not very friendly. Have you upset anyone lately – I feel you have already met. It is a woman about your age, but she has spite about her. I feel that jealousy is very strong in her.'

Cassandra stared at Sabina, dumfounded, wondering who that could be. *Surely it could not be Ruth, the cow that stole my life away. Surely, she wouldn't mess with me. She wouldn't come back, would she? No, she would not dare!*

Sabina continued. 'However, you have the emperor to protect you from harm. Your feelings will become intense in the future for someone – maybe a man – but you will have competition from another woman. It comes as a warning, nothing major, but be on your guard. Things might not appear as they seem. Pay attention to your dreams and intuition because they will come to the fore and help you navigate the future.'

She paused. 'I feel you also have the gift of prophecy and can see and hear spirit. It is there to help you and you should not be afraid.' Beads of sweat trickled into the tiny tramlines etched on her face. Then there was silence; not even the shop seemed to emanate a sound.

Sabina took Cassandra's hand and studied her palm intently. 'Just as I thought, you have the mark of the healer and you definitely have the gift. You also have the mystic cross, which makes you a powerful mystic. Your journey in life is only just beginning.'

She inhaled deeply and continued. 'I feel as though you had to have your broken tower moment because it thrust you onto your true path. You must now follow your destiny. You must develop your skills as a healer and learn to entertain your visions and premonitions.'

She studied Cassandra's eyes. 'Have you ever seen or felt spirit, Cassandra? Do your eyes ever change colour, going paler and softer when you are relaxing?'

'No, I don't think so. Not that I've noticed. And my father always told me that there is a rational explanation for everything.'

'It becomes clear now. Your father taught you to dismiss anything otherworldly as nonsense, but he was only protecting you in his own way. There is always an explanation to these things, but sometimes the rational explanation is of a supernatural nature. I think you have suppressed your natural mystical ability, but that can be changed. Just start to believe in yourself and listen to your intuition. Is your mother sensitive to spirit?'

Cassandra, still feeling a little vulnerable, answered hesitantly, 'I don't know. My mother died when I was four years old.'

'I am sorry to hear that. But they do say the gift is inherited from the mother's side.'

Cassandra admitted, 'My grandmother is a bit weird.'

'On your mother's side?'

'Yes.'

'In what way?'

It was Cassandra who inhaled deeply now, then she composed herself and began her tale. 'She has dreams that she says come true. She swears by them, but we don't believe her really – that is, my father and I don't believe it. However, I can remember her saying once when I was younger that she'd had a dream vision that the police had just caught a serial murderer who was terrorising cities in the north. She described him in detail, right down to the colour of his eyes, which were, as she put it, as black and still as coal. She said he had black hair and a black beard.

'I remember we laughed, but she scoffed at us and said just you wait and see. She told us how he was caught, and a few days later it was in all the papers. The murderer had been captured, but the press had not been informed because the police had to make sure it was their man.

'He was caught in the early hours of the morning and had a large bag of tools with him. A lone policeman apprehended him, thinking he was a burglar. The murderer fell over a garden wall with his heavy bag of killing tools, exactly as my grandmother had described. That spooked me a little because my grandma was spot on.'

'That is very interesting,' said Sabina, wide-eyed.

'My father put the event down to coincidence, and I felt compelled to go along with him. I suppose it was so weird, we didn't want to believe it. We laughed about it, but it did make me think!'

'There you go, Cassandra. Your rational explanation was that your grandmother had the gift of clairvoyance and prophecy.'

Cassandra seemed to be thinking of that event now as credible.

As they walked back into the shop, music infiltrated her senses again, together with the strong, potent sweet aroma that permeated the air.

Sabina put her hand gently on her shoulder. 'If ever you need me or want any advice, you know where I am. You are one of us, Cassandra, and I welcome you to Whalley Dell. Here.' She turned and chose a deep-blue, palm-sized crystal. 'This is a lapis-lazuli crystal and is good to hold for any communication – spirit or otherwise.' She dropped it into Cassandra's palm and closed her fingers tightly around it. 'Wash it under a cold running tap,' she said. 'That will cleanse it and make it yours.'

'Thank you so much,' said Cassandra as she left the shop.

She walked along the high street, feeling lighter. There was a strange glow inside her tummy. Holding her crystal firmly in her hand, she could still feel and smell the delectable fragrance of Magic Things anchoring around her aura.

As she made her way home, she thought of all the moments she'd had in the past that could only have been supernatural in nature. She thought about last night's encounter: was it possible

31

that she might be dealing with a stubborn spirit in her house that had never moved out?

Her mind zinging, and her mouth as dry as sandpaper, she walked along the high street, relieved that Sabina hadn't revealed all of her secret past.

6

Mark the builder plugged his extension lead into the wobbly electric socket and switched on his radio. Music pulsated through the ancient bones of the cottage. Craig was busy knocking off plaster downstairs and making an unbelievable mess.

Mark glanced his way. 'Hey, you better get that plaster cleaned up before she gets back. Get it in the skip. Don't let it build up like that.' He had a rustic face, weather-beaten and raw from a lifetime of mending broken houses.

Craig shovelled up the cracked old plaster that had encased the walls for two hundred years. Like old skin the colour of alabaster, it had fallen from the walls easily, landing in clumps and clouds of dust. Mark had started hacking out the old kitchen units in the back kitchen and they had fallen apart quite easily, tumbling down like dehydrated cardboard. Dust saturated the whole cottage, visibly polluting the air they breathed with grittiness.

Suddenly the radio fell silent; the only noise now came from the annoying squeak of the wheelbarrow as it carried its cargo to the skip out front.

'What's up with the radio now?' complained Mark as he fiddled with the knobs. He tried another socket but there was still nothing. As he grumbled 'Stupid thing!', it suddenly slipped from his hands and crashed on the stone floor. 'Shit.'

He felt a whispering sensation on the back of his head, as though something cold and clingy had landed around his shoulders. He stroked his neck, brushed it away and stepped backwards. He looked up, thinking something had fallen down, but there was nothing above him but ceiling. He was alone in the room.

Hearing movement from the kitchen, he investigated. 'Craig! Is that you?' he shouted into the kitchen, thinking Craig had sneaked up behind him and thrown something cold and clammy at him for a joke. But no; as he looked sideways, he glimpsed Craig, his lanky frame struggling to empty the wheelbarrow out front.

Mark went into the kitchen, expecting a confrontation. He was used to thieves prowling about when he was on site, opportunists who would steal anything that was not nailed down. He remembered one job when he had turned up on site to find two burly men, old enough to know better, thieving stone flags from the back yard and hurling them into a white transit van, the engine still running.

'Who's there? Hello?' he shouted, but the kitchen was empty. He went to the back door and scanned outside. Nothing. *It can't be my imagination.*

As he turned around to walk back into the kitchen, he saw something lurking in the shadows, a movement, then an insipid watery stare. Two eyes were scrutinising him from the grey shadowy corner of the room. The thing appeared to be hunched over, a misty outline of a person.

There was a sudden stillness, as though the air all around had been paralysed. Fear speared his senses as he realised it was a ghostly apparition glaring at him with a wicked stare. Its gaze held him tightly; not once did it leave him, as though it needed to stare at him in order to feed from his life force to maintain its presence in the earthly dimension.

Mark ran outside, carrying the image of the face with its pinprick pupils. Every hair on his body was erect with electrical energy. He remained there, frozen, for what seemed like eternity.

Craig appeared at the back door. 'What's up with the radio?' He noticed Mark's strange demeanour. 'You, okay?'

'Did you see that?' Mark was shaking, his eyes wide, his breathing laboured.

'See what?'

Suddenly the radio spat back to life, pulsating noisily through the air.

Mark didn't believe in ghosts; *a load of bloody rubbish,* he used to think, until today. Screwing the cup from his flask of tea, he sat down on the stone steps among the plentiful weeds and foliage.

Craig was at his side, half-laughing. 'What's up mate? You look like you've seen a ghost.'

Mark glared back at him, unable to get the right words to convey what he had just seen. *He'll think I'm a bloody fool!* The

34

heat of the sun was burning the back of his neck and the music from the radio seemed to dominate, to blaze away and trivialise his experience, bringing him back to reality. *Am I going mad? What do I say to him? Yes, mate, I've just seen a bloody ghost?*

Now, trying to make sense of it, he decided to push the experience far into the void at the back of his mind. He made sure it was buried deep and continued with his work.

'It's okay, lad. I thought I saw someone lurking outside, thieving bastards. I'm just on my guard, that's all. Come on, let's get stuck in. We don't want Cassandra to think we've been sat on our arses all day, do we?'

Filled with anger, and brainwashing himself that the encounter was just his mind playing tricks, he threw his full weight back into the house. *It's my bloody imagination!*

They both got back to work, clearing away the filth and memories two-hundred years had left behind, neither of them realising the presence was still there, waiting, watching and hiding somewhere in the gloomy recesses of the cottage.

***

Cassandra made her way back to her cottage, unaware of the carnage and dusty mess she was about to see. From the road she saw the bright-yellow skip in the front garden. It looked as though it had descended from outer space, its huge mass overshadowing the quaint curb appeal of the house.

The young lanky labourer was manoeuvring a beaten-up metal wheelbarrow almost overflowing with rubble. Walking along the path, her feet crunched over cracked and hacked-up plaster. Mark was at the door forcing a half-smile as she walked slowly towards him. She couldn't control her shock and she didn't realise her mouth was gaping in dismay.

'Hi, Cassandra. This is the worst bit, excavating all the rubbish and crumbling plaster. We'll get that out the way and begin to install your new damp course, then we'll plaster and replace the rotten floorboards. The electrician is coming tomorrow to get the new wiring in, then we'll get the plumber,' he said.

She knew there would be mess – but this? Inside the house, the downstairs rooms had been disembowelled, leaving an almost empty carcass. Motes of dust danced around, enhanced by the intense sunshine that penetrated the window. The ceilings were still in place, though, and she hoped her living quarters upstairs hadn't been disturbed.

Trying not to breathe grit into her lungs, she held her hand over her nose as she climbed the creaking staircase to her bedroom. The door had been opened and her lovely bed was covered in a crispy film of dirt.

I can't live here with all this, I'll go mad, she thought. She decided to pack a bag with essentials and see if she could book into a nearby hotel or B&B. She would go to the café and see if they knew anywhere decent, she could stay for a while.

She felt quite annoyed with the builders, but it wasn't really their fault. She took full responsibility; she should have known better. *What was I thinking of, living here whilst it was being renovated?*

'Hi, Mark, I'm going to book myself into a hotel or B&B. Just carry on. I'll see you later on today and tell you where I am.'

'See you soon, love,' Mark barked, his face still frozen from his earlier encounter. He was hiding it well. Despite his nerves, frazzled by the spectre, he couldn't help but watch her as she strode down the road, her cotton dress flapping slightly in the warm breeze and revealing the gentle feminine curves of her slim, toned body.

7

In the café, Cassandra asked one of the waitresses if she knew of anywhere decent to stay.

'You can try the Green Man, love. Sometimes they have rooms available.'

Cassandra didn't really want to stay in a pub; she'd rather have had somewhere more discreet, where she didn't have to pass through a bar full of brawny men drinking beer every time she went in and out.

'Thanks, I might try them,' she said.

'It's not star accommodation, though,' the waitress added.

That convinced her not to try there – it might be worse than roughing it at the cottage.

It was nearly lunchtime and Cassandra ordered a pot of tea and a ploughman's sandwich. Taking a seat outside, she observed the leisurely meanderings along the high street. Across the road Magic Things was still open, a few people coming out of the entrance. She decided to pop in there and see if Sabina knew of anywhere, she could stay.

Manoeuvring across the street, she felt sticky and hot. The sun was bearing down on her and the tarmac underfoot felt bouncy, spongy, as though it were melting. Inside the shop, a portable fan on the counter cooled the fragranced air and offered welcome relief. She felt the perspiration on her body begin to evaporate.

Sabina was behind the counter with Charity; they were both laughing as they talked. Cassandra slowly approached and they stopped and looked in her direction.

'Hi, Cassandra, is everything okay?' asked Sabina. 'You're not upset by the reading earlier, I hope?' She came round the counter.

'No of course not. The thing is, I'm looking for somewhere to stay. You know my house is being renovated. When I went back, I realised I can't live there at the moment. There's dust everywhere, and I can't breathe. I didn't expect such a mess!'

Sabina sighed sympathetically. 'I think we all underestimate how much dust a house can cough up when it's being repaired. Have you tried the Green Man? They do rooms – but it might be full, this being nearly holiday season.'

'I don't really want to stay there. I need a bit of privacy, and it might be too noisy.' Cassandra sighed again.

Charity came over. 'I was just listening to you,' she said. She looked at her mother. 'Mum, what about the caravan in the meadow? That's empty – she could stay there.'

'What?' said Sabina. There was a cold silence, as if Charity had just betrayed one of her mother's deepest, darkest secrets. A faraway look glazed her green eyes as she said, 'That's my pride and joy. It's been in the family for decades. I don't know, you probably wouldn't like it anyway.' She shrugged her shoulders at Cassandra.

Then there was that cold silence again. Cassandra, sensing the tension and feeling awkward, cut through it. 'Please, no, I don't want to intrude. You don't have to let me stay there.' She imagined an old smelly caravan, dilapidated and with no functioning facilities, a leaking roof and an old bucket outside to carry water. God knows where she would go to the toilet!

Charity said, with the naive tact of a typical teenager, 'You don't mind, do you, Mum? The extra money would come in handy.'

Sabina said reluctantly, 'I suppose you can have a look. I'll have to charge the going rate.'

Cassandra didn't want to look. She didn't want to stay in an old caravan – she'd rather stay in her own back-garden shed – but now she was caught up in a tangled web and felt obliged to look. She decided she would visit it and think of a plausible excuse to decline it.

Leaving Charity in the shop, Sabina and Cassandra went to see the gypsy caravan. One o'clock sunshine glazed the meadow, displaying the abundant tapestry of wild flowers. A meandering path wove through it, shadowed by the long grass on either side.

The caravan looked nice from a distance, and bigger than she'd expected. As she got closer and its full glory was revealed, a strong curiosity took hold of her.

It was an antique, wooden bow-top gypsy caravan with steps at the front leading to a porch. An exquisite pattern in cream and pastel green adorned it, and it was dotted all over with little white flowers. Large stones anchored the wheels.

'Wow, it's beautiful! I never imagined anything like this,' sighed Cassandra.

'This is my horse-drawn Romani wagon. She is beautiful, isn't she?'

The roof was made of teal canvas. A little black chimney peeped through its smooth surface.

'It doesn't go anywhere these days, but I've been on the road with it many times in the past. Since my dappled shire horse, Grey, died, I've left the caravan in the field. It's somewhere I retreat to when I need space and focus, but I don't mind you staying here for a while, especially if you can't find anywhere else. You're new to the village and I'd love to help you in any way I can.'

'Thank you, that's so kind of you.' Cassandra was keen to look inside. She knew she was very privileged to be allowed to stay there; it was a private, special place for Sabina and no doubt held a lot of memories.

She noticed a handful of cottages in the distance, their gardens overlooking the meadow. Each one had a little garden gate with access to the path.

'I live over there.' Sabina pointed towards them. 'It's the one on the far end, so if you need anything you know where we are. But you can see us in the shop during the day and we're open most days till late.'

Cassandra hovered by the entrance to the caravan. 'Can I go in?' she asked.

'Yes, of course. It might not suit your needs but have a look.' Sabina waited on the porch so as not to crowd her.

Cassandra paused by the entrance, surveying everything with unspoken wonder. She felt as if she had been transported into a fairy tale. She entered, treading lightly over ash-grey wooden floor. The interior gleamed with cream paint, and there was a small cream-coloured shaker-style kitchen on the right of her, which led to a cushioned seating area. To her left, there was a little foldaway table with two small chairs and a black stove in the corner.

The windows either side were dressed in pastel-coloured roman blinds. Ahead of her was an array of cream storage units and drawers, in the middle of which was the cosiest bed she had ever seen, made up with a pink, blue and yellow patchwork quilt. At the rear above the bed was another window with a dusky-blue blind.

The interior basked in sunshine from the little windows. Aromatic candles had been placed on some surfaces, and the caravan smelt of fresh soap and essential oils.

Cassandra had never seen anything so beautiful and immaculate. She felt ashamed of her preconceptions; this was the absolute opposite of what she had expected. How could she have doubted its suitability?

Sabina nudged past her and said with a hint of pride, 'You haven't seen this yet.' She opened a full-length cupboard on the left and inside was a cute shower room with a toilet.

'Wow, it's amazing! You would let me stay here?' asked Cassandra.

'Yes, if you like. I use it every now and then to get away from the world. Its far enough away from civilization for me to pretend to live my bohemian lifestyle.' She laughed. 'I love to escape here once in a while and pretend I'm in a fictional wonderland. I suppose it is quite child-like. Charity calls it my Wendy house, but I don't care – I love it.'

'This really is lovely. I'd love to take it, but only if you are absolutely sure. I promise I will look after it. I'll only need it for a week or two.'

'It has electricity too,' added Sabina.

Cassandra's stomach fluttered with excitement. 'That's fantastic,'

'I nearly forgot.' Sabina opened another cupboard beside the table, exposing a small TV. 'I will expect payment up front for two-weeks' stay.' Her tone was more serious now, and she looked deep into Cassandra's golden eyes. 'I know I can trust you. I know I can!'

Cassandra felt blessed that she was being given the opportunity to stay in such a magical place. She smiled. 'Yes,

Sabina, you can trust me. I will treat this place with respect, I won't disappoint you.'

She half-ran back to her cottage to get her belongings. She hadn't noticed that, behind the caravan in the distance and beyond the clearing, the snaking path continued its journey straight into the dark knotted mass of Dead Man's Wood.

***

'I'll leave the key with you, Mark. Is that okay?' Cassandra asked. She was keen to return with the money for Sabina.

Mark didn't tell her about the ghost, even though he couldn't forget it no matter how hard he tried. He couldn't tell her; besides making him look daft, it might un-nerve her and she might decide not to move in after all and sell the place. He needed the work. Women could be funny with that sort of thing.

He took the key from her, promising he would lock up each day.

'If you need me call me,' she said.

'Okay, love! See yah!' He just wanted to get the job done as quickly as possible, get paid and go. *Bloody weird house!*

8

Cassandra settled into the caravan that evening and sat on the wooden steps, watching the sun melt into the horizon. Feeling sleepy, she washed, then looked closer into the shower-room mirror to see if her eyes were changing colour like Sabina had suggested. She inhaled some deep breaths to relax herself, then looked again. She couldn't see any difference in colour, although maybe the flecks of gold were more profound?

Tucking herself into the cosy bed, she drifted in and out of sleep. The air was muggy and kept clawing her awake, but within twenty minutes she was slumbering. It wasn't long before she awoke again with a start. She could hear something outside, a rustling movement: someone was prowling about.

'Hello, who's that?' She switched on the lamps and went to the entrance. 'Hello, who's there?'

There was nothing but silence. Reluctantly she made her way back to bed, leaving the lights on to bathe the interior with a soft golden glow. Was she alone in a solitary, bow-top gypsy caravan, isolated, illuminated like a lantern in the midnight meadow? A silhouette against the backdrop of Dead Man's Wood?

***

That day, Ruben Capricornus had followed Cassandra to her new lodgings, scrutinising her every movement whilst concealing himself within the twisted mass of Dead Man's Wood. As darkness fell, he watched the illuminated caravan and waited until the lantern glow from inside was no more.

He prowled stealthily across the meadow until he was at the rear of the caravan, concealed in the shadows. The moonlight was teasing sparkles against the shimmering paint, making it look otherworldly in its ripe and fertile surroundings.

He could sense Cassandra inside and thought that maybe he was only a few inches away from her scantily-clad body. The thought of it sent a siren of arousal through his perfectly toned masculinity. Pressing the side of his waxy face gently against the panel where he knew her bed was, he closed his devil-like eyes and gently inhaled the pleasure of his sudden stimulation.

He stroked his long fingers against the iridescent paint, wondering if he was almost touching her naked flesh. He sighed silently. Would she be his conquest? Did she have a sinful heart? Oh, he hoped so, otherwise his enchantment would not work on her. To find a witch without a pure heart was rare… Just one sin – just one – was all he needed. Then he could seduce her and make her his own forever

But he wasn't sure yet. His erotic stimulation subsided. He would know when the time was right – but not yet.

His ghostly white skin reflected the moonlight as it accompanied him across the meadow and into the woods. Statuesque but spritely, his figure almost pranced then dissolved into the darkness beyond.

***

Before long, it was morning and sunshine was streaming through the little windows. Although she felt the anxiety of last night's prowler, amazingly it hadn't interfered with Cassandra's sleep. Maybe it had not been a prowler, just her imagination spooking her.

Having slept so soundly, she was unwilling to get up such was the hypnotic effect of her new temporary lodging. The calm interior was warming up nicely from the abundant early sunshine. Today she would explore the meadow and its surroundings, but first she would make her way to the café in the village to have breakfast.

After showering, she trudged along the path to the café on the high street. The air was sweet with the promise of another hot day. After a light snack of fruit, bread and tea, she followed the path to the caravan back across the meadow. Suddenly she stopped and looked at the horizon and the black mass of Dead Man's Wood. If she followed the snaking path, it would lead her into its unfamiliar void. A wash of uneasiness reddened her cheeks and her stomach churned.

She remembered what Saffron had said about it being so big she would easily get lost, and she had also said it was private.

Why? She noticed a cluster of people entering the meadow from the wood, as though it were a public right of way. Then she remembered what Saffron had said about wolves prowling its dark recesses; had the girl been trying to frighten her?

She watched as the happy family moved across the meadow, following a path on the edge of the wood. Then, disturbingly, in the distance she saw the hazy figure of a man, unmoving, watching her. She turned around, thinking he was staring at something behind her, but there was nothing there.

When she looked back, the figure had vanished. How could he have done that so quickly? Surely, she would have seen him re-entering the woods or walking away? The sun dazzled her vision and she realised she was alone in the meadow; the family had turned the corner into the distance, making their way to the high street.

Maybe renting the caravan wasn't such a good idea after all? She felt like an easy target for creeps and weirdos. She looked over to Sabina's house with its open garden gate, its abundant foliage almost spilling out into the meadow, then she looked back to where the figure had been standing and felt a shiver run down her spine. She decided to go to Magic Things, ask Sabina about the area and tell her what she had seen.

Strolling across the meadow, Cassandra turned around occasionally to see if the figure was following her. Her familiar anxiety was creeping back, reminding her of how it could cripple her senses and infiltrate her mind with fear-induced hysteria. She breathed deeply into her lungs, letting the meadow-sweet air dissolve her fears. She was stronger now than before she had come to Whalley Dell, and she wouldn't let a few unfounded fears get to her. Her humour and common sense were energising her with confidence; she was in control, wasn't she?

When she entered the shop, it was empty of customers and Sabina and Charity were having a well-deserved cup of tea. It was nearly lunchtime and the café across the road was heaving with people trying to get tables and seats. Cassandra smiled with relief that the shop wasn't busy, but she didn't quite know how to word what she was about to say. Hesitating slightly, she asked, 'Are there any weirdos around here?'

Sabina and Charity looked at each other and started laughing. Pulling a face, Charity asked, 'Why? has anyone been bothering you?'

'No, it's just that I felt a little bit strange on my own at the caravan last night. I thought I heard someone prowling about outside.'

Sabina looked at her curiously. 'I don't think so. I've been living here all my life and the locals are alright. Some might be a bit fruity, but they're harmless.'

Charity cut in, 'Mum, what about Bill the tramp? He's a bit odd!'

'Yes, but he's harmless – just a sad old drunk.' The mystical music breathed its mood into the shop. 'No, you're safe around here, although I can only speak for the locals. I can't vouch for the tourists.'

Cassandra said, 'When I was leaving the caravan earlier, I looked towards Dead Man's Wood and saw a strange figure of a man in the distance, staring at me. And then...' she suddenly felt silly '...then he disappeared.'

Sabina tried to calm her. 'Sometimes you can feel a bit vulnerable staying in a strange place, especially a caravan in the middle of a field on your own. It's Friday, and we usually go to the pub across the road after dinner for a drink. Why don't you come to the house, then we can all go and get to know each other a little better? I don't want you to feel vulnerable or isolated. And you can meet some of the locals. What do you think?'

With nothing to lose, Cassandra agreed.

They met up at 7pm then strolled across the meadow to the Green Man. Its sign was not moving; there was no breeze, just a suffocating staleness that held everything taut and muggy.

Inside the pub it was even warmer, and the many customers milling around the bar moved the stagnating heat around. They took a table by an open window, hoping to get respite from a breeze, but none obliged.

Sabina went to the bar for a bottle of Chardonnay and three glasses. The landlord, Frank, followed her back carrying the wine in a frosted ice bucket that was weeping profusely with condensation.

Sabina filled their glasses and Cassandra felt the coolness of the wine travel down her throat, numbing her anxiety. She moistened her brow and the nape of her neck with some of the wetness from the bottle and smiled. It might be a good idea to enquire about Dead Man's Wood. She wondered if Saffron had told the truth about it being private property. She wouldn't say anything about the wolves, though – they would think her really gullible.

Sabina laughed. 'No, it is not private property. Who told you that?'

'Saffron.'

'Saffron who works here?'

Cassandra nodded.

'Why did she tell you that? It's been a public right of way for many years and anyone can visit. There are legends that witches still live there in tiny houses made of wooden sticks and mud, tending to their bubbling cauldrons of dead frogs, newts and all sorts of nasty things, but that's just folklore.'

Cassandra, still not reassured, asked, 'Who was the man I saw at the entrance of Dead Man's Wood? I know it wasn't my imagination.' She swallowed another sip of her wine.

Sabina stared at her intently. 'It might not have been a man at all.'

'It was definitely a man.'

Sabina moved her head closer to Cassandra. 'No, what I mean is that it might not have been of this world.'

'What do you mean?'

Charity cut in clumsily, 'I think she is trying to tell you it was a ghost. Sometimes we see wild deer, but you have to go very early for that. I can take you tomorrow morning. Are you up for it? That's alright, isn't it, Mum? You can manage for an hour without me, can't you?'

Cassandra was confused at how the conversation had suddenly changed. 'What do you mean it might have been a ghost? It was a man!'

Sabina finished her wine, condensation moistening her fingers. 'Ghosts are seen in all shapes and sizes. Sometimes you can think you are looking at a real person, only for them to disappear in front of your eyes. They don't all appear as white,

46

floaty, misty things.' Pouring another full glass, she added, 'Sometimes it is hard to tell if someone is of this world or the spirit world. Spirits cannot hurt you, Cassandra, only the living.'

'Why did I see it?'

'Like I told you yesterday, you are one of us. I saw the evidence in your palm.' She took Cassandra's hand again and pointed out the cross sign engraved on her palm. 'You were born with the gift of healing and prophecy. With it comes a strong sensitivity to see spirit.' She told her daughter to fetch another bottle from the bar.

Cassandra didn't know what to think, yet somehow it made sense, as though a knowingness had come about her.

She hadn't noticed Saffron behind the bar; she hadn't been there when they had arrived. Trying to catch her eye, Cassandra waved, but Saffron turned away, snubbing her. *What have I done? I must have done something to upset her.*

Saffron seemed to be chatting quite intimately to a man at the other side of the bar. He was young and extremely good looking, and his hair was thick and glossy black. Cassandra could tell Saffron was flirting with him. Maybe it was her boyfriend.

Saffron looked at Cassandra again then quickly looked away. The man noticed and turned around. Cassandra, trying to conceal a blush, looked down at her glass as she felt his eyes on her. There was a roar of laughter; he and Saffron seemed to be sharing a joke at her expense.

Sabina noticed them laughing and said, 'Do you know Fenton? Have you seen him before?'

'No, but I feel like I'm being laughed at,' said Cassandra, intimidated by their amusement.

'No! he's not like that. I'll introduce you, if you like.' Sabina stood up and her stool scraped against the stone-flagged floor.

Cassandra snapped, 'No, don't!' but it was too late. Sabina was on her feet, going to the bar. Charity came back to the table with the fresh bottle of wine and began to pour another glass.

Then he was there, bending over Cassandra, his fresh face wearing a shy grin. 'Hi, I'm Fenton ... Fenton Brooks,' he said. 'Sabina wants to introduce us.'

Sabina cut in. 'This is Cassandra, she's new in the village. She's bought the old cottage up the road on Meadow Row.'

47

'The one that's all run down?' he enquired curiously. His voice was smooth, warm and steady. 'Nice to meet you, Cassandra.'

'Nice to meet you,' replied Cassandra, taking his hand. She could feel its polished leathery texture and knew he must be a manual worker. Suppressing an unwelcome shyness, she enquired, 'Do you live around here?'

He smiled. 'I'm helping out up at Saffron's old man's place, but I live in the next village, Corston. Brooks Farm, do you know it?'

'No, everywhere is new to me around here. It's still a bit of an adventure.'

'But we're going to the woods tomorrow morning to have a look around, aren't we?' Charity said.

'Ooh! The spooky wood!' he laughed. He had nice white teeth. Glancing at the bar, he said goodbye and claimed his seat across from Saffron, who was pulling at the beer pump.

Cassandra noticed the girl scowl at her before serving another customer. A lot of people were staring at her, as though she had grown two heads. 'Why do I feel like I'm on show for some reason?' she asked.

Sabina laughed. 'It is just the way they are around here. Word has probably got round that you've bought the old cottage and they're curious, that's all.'

Two men walked in from the beer garden. One had short, spiky red hair; the other was taller and slimmer, with short brown hair. They sauntered over to Fenton and started talking.

'Are those Saffron's brothers?' Cassandra asked.

Sabina glanced over. 'Yes, that's Sam with the red hair, and the other one is Joe. Have you met them?'

'No, but I met Saffron when I got lost on a walk. She steered me back to the village and mentioned her brothers. She seems to be snubbing me.'

'Saffron? She's harmless enough. She's one of us, a mystic. She comes in the shop for supplies every now and then.'

'What kind of supplies?'

'Oh, the usual ones – prairie sage, candles, crystals. She dabbles in the cards, too.'

Sam had a look of his sister, but in all the wrong ways. He had a heavy jawline and, when he turned around, his eyes were deep set and moody. His brother Joe looked tamer and was better looking. She wondered if they all had the same father.

There was more laughter at the bar as Sam and Joe turned around to look in their direction. Cassandra wondered what was making them laugh so much and felt slightly paranoid by the atmosphere that permeated the place.

Charity groaned. 'We'll go in a minute. Some of them give me the creeps, too!'

As they walked to the exit, Sabina smiled and waved confidently to the crowd at the bar. 'Goodnight, folks!' she said. Then everyone looked at Cassandra, most of the men undressing her with their eyes, including Joe and Sam. Only Fenton didn't; he gazed into her eyes and said gently, 'Goodnight Cassandra.'

That night, when the moon settled into its black sky and all was quiet, Cassandra could not get the image of Fenton Brooks out of her mind. Gone were all the regrets of the past, her ex-fiancé and all the turmoil that went with him; it was as though they had dissolved away. However, she was annoyed, so very annoyed that she couldn't stop thinking about Fenton.

From her pillow she glanced out of the window to the moonlit sky and watched a shooting star slice across the heavens. Its long silver trail glinted as bright as diamonds, then disappeared into the night behind the hooded horizon of Dead Man's Wood.

9

The innocent morning birthed itself into the day under a blanching sunrise. Cassandra sat watching the warm breeze whipping across the meadows, stroking the profusion of wild flowers into waves.

She opened the porch door of her gypsy retreat and inhaled the fresh, sweet air, stretching her arms into the purity the morning had gifted. Inside, she made some coffee and breakfasted on croissants and fruit. She was ready to become acquainted with Dead Man's Wood and her heart fluttered in anticipation.

A familiar face entered the caravan; it was Charity, her long hair wispy in the breeze, her blue eyes eager and happy. 'Are you decent?' she asked, putting her water flask on the kitchen worktop.

'Yes, come in, Charity. Would you like some coffee, a croissant, perhaps?'

'Ooh, lovely. Yes, please.' She smelt of fresh linen and lavender soap. Her hair was tied back revealing her flawless complexion. Her rosy cheeks, sparkling with a whisper of blusher, betrayed her youth.

It was nine o'clock when they ventured into Dead Man's Wood, too late to see any wild deer but too early for the zealous sun to disturb them. Cassandra wanted to eradicate any unfounded fears she harboured about the area.

They strode along the dusty dry path, Cassandra with her long gypsy dress flapping and gently cooling her legs, and Charity wearing loose cotton shorts and a T-shirt. They chatted happily along the way.

They entered the shadowy depths of Dead Man's Wood and followed a meandering path of broken twigs, their legs brushing against the array of ferns and lavish foliage. Their thoughts surrendered to its wild intelligence, as though the sudden entrance into its abyss had intensified their vision and amplified their senses. A heady scent of honeysuckle and a flurry of delicate white bells of lily-of-the-valley offered a silent welcome. It was not unlike entering a gothic cathedral, its lofty heights not stone but a canopy of intricate branches that emitted diamond-like shimmers of light, activating the fertile life beneath.

Cassandra sighed with joy. She bent down slowly to pick some clusters of wild flowers made up of purple studs with little white petals. Charity harvested some, too; as she bent over, strands of hair came loose and floated annoyingly onto her face and eyes. She tucked it back behind her ears.

Cassandra felt as though she'd been transported into another dimension – then she caught a movement in her peripheral vision. She thought she'd seen something move in the darkest shadows, but she could have been mistaken.

Stopping, she turned around, but there was nothing, nothing but an empty path snaking back into the meadow. An earthy odour of dampness accompanied a misty trail of morning dew, which was rising now to a ghostly fog, like dancing drapes of pure white silk, sliding horizontally in slow motion.

Not too perturbed, she looked around for more wild flowers. Sticking to the path, not wanting to get lost, they walked alongside a brook framed on both sides by hectic undergrowth. Its bed had almost been dried up by the greedy heat of summer. In places it had become stagnant and pooled like thick green soup.

Birdsong accompanied them deep into the woods. As they strode over dismembered branches and twigs, cracks echoed into the space around them. They didn't realise that they were being followed from a distance.

Suddenly they noticed a strong odour of burning wood coming from the deep recesses of the wood. Plumes of smoke were rising like powdery grey strands, writhing through the trees; it made them gag.

Charity complained first. 'Oh my God, someone has lit a fire over there!' She pointed into the tall trees that had never been tamed by a pathway. Continuing her rant, she exclaimed, 'That is so annoying. Some people have no respect. You're not supposed to light fires in the woods. Come on, let's see where it's coming from.'

In single file, with Charity in front, they strayed from the path and tackled the knotted undergrowth, plunging themselves deeper into its wild clutches.

***

Ruben Capricornus watched them enter Dead Man's Wood. He had concealed himself in a grove of trees, then cautiously let his instincts take over and guide him. He wanted to introduce himself. He kept a safe distance, and, when he saw them detour from the regular path, he prowled away from it to where he could creep up and watch them from a distance. He didn't know what his next move would be, but something deep and perverse was animating him. He knew these woods intimately so he would watch them from afar.

But what was this? He could smell smoke up ahead. Realising that someone else might be there, he turned around and sped out of the wood. He didn't want to be found, didn't want confrontation. He would wait until the women were alone.

As he navigated out of the woods, he saw the gypsy caravan in the distance, quiet and alone in the meadow, shimmering in the heat. It wasn't his fault, he *had* to do it... He paused next to it and urinated onto its wheels, the straw-coloured liquid splashing around his feet, then pooling onto the dry earth.

He sauntered along the meadow path. As if he were having an innocent morning stroll, he emerged onto the main road of Whalley Dell, where he disappeared back into the ether, dissolving into the clusters of pedestrians, vehicles and shoppers along the high street.

10

It wasn't long before they both came across a clearing and a sinister abode, a sort of cottage. The rickety wooden structure with a slatted roof had a fat chimney, not unlike a tall crown. Spirals of pale grey smoke rose from it into the surrounding gloomy haziness. The cottage seemed to be hiding from the rest of the world like a fugitive, concealing itself in a long-forgotten space.

Two glossy black crows flew down, perched next to the chimney and squawked in unison, their shrill alarm piercing the air as though alerting whoever was inside of danger. But then something strange happened; it became eerily cold, so cold as to cause unseasonal goose bumps and shivers.

Instinctively Cassandra rubbed her arms. 'God, it is so cold. Can the sun not reach this part?'

'I know, I'm feeling it too. My legs are freezing. That's probably why someone has lit a fire in there!'

They moved hesitantly closer, curious to see more; neither of them had seen any place like this before. 'What the...?' Charity was stuck for words, and they looked at each other with disbelief.

'Where is this?' Cassandra asked, automatically thinking Charity would know.

'I have no idea,' the girl half-whispered. 'I didn't know it existed and I've lived here all my life.'

It didn't help to calm them, and they were both hesitant to find out who lived in such a place. They were about to edge back but noticed a small, silhouetted figure of a bony woman with a mass of grey, wiry hair standing in the doorway. She had a long clay pipe jutting out of her tight mouth, gently held by almost skeletal fingers. She looked absolutely filthy, so much so that her skin was not visible; she was encased in a crusty layer of dirt. Only the whites of her eyes gleamed.

She began to talk to them. Her voice was as sharp as cut glass and loud, her dialect hardly decipherable. 'Yes? What you want with me, lass?' Her mouth was almost devoid of teeth and she sucked noisily on her pipe.

'We are just passing through.' Cassandra automatically said the first words that came to her. She was keen to turn and hurry back to the path again.

The woman glared at them inquisitively. 'Come on now, what you want? You shouldn't be in these woods alone. It's a bad place, bad! You're here for something. What do you want?' She moved slowly towards them, her sapphire-blue eyes squinting with curiosity. 'Don't be shy.'

Charity and Cassandra locked eyes, not knowing what to say. They began to slowly walk backwards into the dense thicket from whence they had come.

'No, it's all right, we don't want anything... We...' said Charity.

'Ye tell nothing about me, you hear me? Don't ye tell on me or I'll get you!' The old woman's tone changed and her eyes grew as wide as boiled eggs.

Cassandra and Charity talked over each other, swearing that they would not tell. Cassandra finished with, 'You can trust us.'

'Trust? Trust? I trust no one!' the woman said. Waving her hand and swatting it into the smoky air between them, she said, 'You just go away. You've no business with me. Go now! Go...!'

She turned her back on them and went inside her miserable dwelling, mumbling her annoyance.

Cassandra and Charity quickly navigated the rough terrain back to the familiar path. Neither of them spoke. Their breathing was laboured as they fled from the woods, their frantic running accompanied by an eerie noise of echoing cracks and rustling foliage.

They got back to the trail leading to the meadow, but something strange had happened. The air was still cold and unseasonal, and it held a subtle new vibration. No leaves adorned the trees and the ground they walked on was hard as ice. A grey sky as heavy as marble had descended and swallowed up the sun.

They watched their breath penetrate the cold air and realised they were both shivering. Entering the meadow from the wood, they hoped to see the gypsy caravan in its cluster of wild flowers – but it wasn't there. Everything had been replaced by knotted grass with a silvery layer of frost upon it. The sky was low and claustrophobic, and the ground hard as steel. They could no longer see any movement along the high street in the distance, and the telephone and electricity cables had vanished.

Charity looked towards the row of cottages and the house in which she lived, but it was very different. All the chimneys were spewing out long streams of blackened smoke, polluting the sky to a deep shade of purple-grey.

'What is this? Charity, I don't understand!' Cassandra said, scanning the area with disbelief.

'I don't bloody know. What the hell?'

Then as quickly as it had gone, like the subtle ripple of a pebble dropping into a pond, the familiar world came back. The summer sun reclaimed the sky and shone its welcome warmth upon them, and their shivering skin ached with relief.

They found themselves standing upon the dry path looking at the gypsy caravan. As though on auto pilot, they silently navigated across the field. It was as though their own senses could not accept what they had just seen and no words would come.

Once at the caravan, they went inside, sat down and stared at one another. They were both thinking the same thing: that they were utterly confused. Cassandra broke the silence first. 'What happened just then?'

Although it felt as though they'd been in the wood for only half an hour, the digital clock on the cooker showed that three hours had passed and it was lunch time.

Charity, wide eyed, asked, 'Was that real?'

'It was not a dream,' Cassandra said, in a hushed voice. 'We both witnessed this. What is this strange village – this strange world – I've ended up in?'

11

After a coffee and an attempt to come up with a reasonable explanation, they realised they could not. They had slipped into some kind of mysterious time-warp. They could not shake off the shivery memory and it clawed at their rational minds, eager for an explanation. Their encounter in Dead Man's Wood was not of this century.

Cassandra was disturbed by the event. The main purpose of exploring the wood was to dispel its mystery and her fears. The opposite had happened and she didn't know whether to laugh or cry.

Charity started to laugh, slowly at first and then almost hysterically. 'I need to tell Mum, she'll be amazed.'

Still feeling shivers from what had happened, Cassandra cut in. 'Who was that woman? Nobody lives like that these days.'

Charity gave a sinister smile. 'I think we've just had a weird encounter and entered into another dimension. I have heard Mum talk of things like this. It's the quantum world, and modern scientists are only just coming to terms with it. The "rational" mind can't understand it – and maybe it never will – but it does exist.'

Cassandra was intrigued, although her face was set like stone. 'Please, Charity, can you stay with me in the caravan? I don't want to be alone here. It's freaked me out a bit.'

'Course I will,' Charity soothed, 'We'll go and see Mum. Maybe she can shed some light on what happened.'

'This is crazy, Charity! I've moved to a crazy village! Am I going mad?'

'You'll get used to it. Things are never as they seem here – but I must admit that was really strange, even for me.'

They strolled to the high street where Saturday shoppers were mulling around and traffic was competing for parking spaces. It was a welcome, familiar scene of reality.

When they told Sabina about the wood, she didn't laugh. Her green eyes widened with acknowledgement, and she slowly nodded to Charity. 'You have finally seen her, too?' she asked, a gentle smile on her lips.

'You mean you know of her?' asked Charity.

'Yes, I have. I saw her many years ago. They call her the Hag of Dead Man's Wood and they say she appears not for malicious reasons to scare people, but to protect the wood and its inhabitants. There is always a trigger that makes her materialise. Some say she warns people of impending danger, but I'm not really sure. Very strange. I'd like to go back there with you this afternoon. You can show me what you saw and where.'

'No, I really don't want to go there again,' Cassandra blurted,

'Don't be afraid... I need to meditate in the back for a while. Can you take over, Charity?' Sabina asked. She seemed to be going into a strange daze. She whispered, 'You must have triggered a quantum moment where strange energies let you slip into her world. I can't explain it, nobody can. It just happens, that's all.'

Chilling silence descended, allowing the melodic tones of otherworldly music to pulsate through the shop and overtake the quietness. Charity stared wide-eyed at her mother, and watched her sidestep customers as she retreated to the back room and closed the door gently behind her.

Charity remained in the shop, serving the handful of customers, and Cassandra stayed with her. Half an hour later, Sabina emerged from the back looking refreshed and ready for action.

She gently touched Cassandra's arm. 'Listen, this is all new to you but you must not be afraid. We will confront it together and maybe you will find that it is just a normal event in life. You are one of us, remember, and you need to learn. Maybe this happened to you for a reason, to propel you on the road to your destiny. You are in control. If at any time you do not want to continue, say so and it will stop.

'You have entered into the next dimension of this earthy reality that many run away from through unfounded fear. It is real, it is happening, and it is part of our spiritual evolution to embrace it. It cannot harm you, only the living can physically hurt us. We, as spiritual warriors, are in control. God, the angels, the universe, whatever you choose to call them, are there for you and you must trust their protection. Goodness and faith are the same in any creed or religion.'

***

Later, when the shop quietened, Sabina closed for a couple of hours and all three went into the Green Man across the road. The pub garden greeted them with a lush green expanse of lawn, dotted with tables. Speedily they claimed one under the generous shelter of an ancient oak tree at the rear of the garden that offered protection from the obstinate heat.

Next to them was a tall tree stump which had been intricately carved into a weird prancing man. Clusters of leaves tumbled around him and his naked body seemed to twist and writhe. The statue had been washed by deep-green wood stain; his squinting eyes had been painted blue and complimented his wide smile. His face looked similar to the squeaky pub sign out front.

All around, diners were eating at tables sheltered by bright yellow umbrellas. There was a cheerful symphony of clattering knives and forks, chiming crockery and indecipherable conversations, interspersed with rising laughter. Cassandra was feeling calmer now and they ordered lunch. The air was alive with delicious aromas from the pub kitchen.

Charity was hungry. 'I'm having chips.'

Cassandra studied the menu. 'I think I'll have a cheese salad – with chips, too.' As she glanced around, there he was again sitting at one of the tables, slightly concealed by the shadow of the umbrella. Fenton Brooks.

He was in conversation with two other heavily-built men, no doubt treating themselves to a hearty lunch and an innocent pint. Feeling her stomach somersault, Cassandra was annoyed that he could have so much control over her. She had sworn off men for the foreseeable future.

Sabina and Charity were chatting about something, but she paid no heed to it; her attention had been ambushed by his presence.

'So, what do you think Cassandra?' asked Sabina.

Cassandra was in a daze as if he were magnetically pulling her towards him. 'Sorry … what was that?' Her confusion was obvious to them and annoying to her.

They automatically followed her gaze and Sabina smiled. 'Oh, look, there's Fenton.' She waved, shouted a greeting to him and all three men looked in their direction.

Cassandra could feel herself blushing again but, not wanting to seem prudish, waved too. He was looking at her now, smiling with that boyish grin, those sultry eyes.

'He's a nice-looking lad, isn't he?' Sabina said.

Cassandra replied uncomfortably, 'Yes, I'm afraid he is. He is too nice!' She watched the waitress approach for their order, a frail girl who looked too young for the job,

They all laughed. As Charity placed her order, Cassandra wondered if Sabina knew her secret thoughts about him.

'I'll put a word in for you, if you like?' Sabina said cheekily, her green eyes glossy in the sunlight.

'No, there's no need. He's with Saffron, isn't he?' Cassandra asked.

'I think she has a crush on him, but they're just friends. I'm sure he's single. I've never seen them on a date or anything like that.'

Cassandra felt a wash of excitement at the thought of having him all to herself. Then he and his workmates stood up and she watched his broad shoulders disappear around the corner. She felt irritated not to be in charge of her emotions. How could she let this man rule her? How dare he? But how could she stop it?

Determined never to be taken for a fool again she said, 'Men like him should be put away. They're a danger to the female race. He must think he's God's gift! Irresistible, or something!'

Sabina began to laugh. 'It's just the way the world is. He can't help it.'

Cassandra laughed too as she realised her error: she had revealed strong feelings for him to Charity and Sabina, otherwise she wouldn't have cared so much.

Charity, noticing the waitress bringing their lunch wasn't the frail girl who had taken their order, said, 'Saffron is bringing our order.'

'Hiya. There you go.' Saffron distributed the food and delicious steaming aromas teased the air.

'Saffron, I'm glad you're here,' said Sabina. 'I need some information.' The atmosphere suddenly became tense.

Saffron waved a fly from her flushed face. 'Yes? What?'

'You know about the hag of Dead Man's Wood, don't you?'

'What about her?' Her tone was relaxed and unconcerned.

'Well, you've seen her, haven't you? In the woods? Have you seen her recently?'

'Why? What do you want with her?' Saffron asked.

Cassandra couldn't believe they were conversing as if the old woman were a normal person of this world.

'What's she been up to lately?' Sabina asked.

'I don't know. She comes and goes when she pleases. Why?' Saffron looked towards the kitchen door, impatient to get back to work.

'Oh, nothing. It's just that she appeared to Cassandra and Charity in the woods today.'

'Really?' Saffron looked to Cassandra with a twinge of disbelief. 'Why would she do that?'

'I don't know, but I think something sinister is brewing in that wood. Something dark and twisted enough to summon her presence into our dimension. And we need to find out what that is.'

Saffron's eyes were still focused on Cassandra.

'Listen,' said Sabina. 'Can you keep a lookout.'

'Yes, of course.' Saffron looked to the kitchen door again. 'I'll have to go, we're busy.'

As they tucked into their pub lunch, Cassandra watched Saffron return to the kitchen. The girl stopped and paused at the threshold to look back at her, then turned and dissolved into the dark shadows.

Sabina, reading Cassandra's demeanour, said, 'I feel the pain of the past isn't quite dealt with, is it? You are still harbouring a deep distrust of men, which is understandable considering what you had to endure. Don't let the pain of the past rule your future, though. Let it go. It wasn't your fault.' Their eyes met and Cassandra felt calmer but still annoyed for letting the past eat away at her.

Charity was curious. 'What happened in your past Cassandra?'

Sabina quickly took over the conversation. 'Charity, we all have past issues, especially with men. Maybe you're not old enough yet to have much experience in the matter.'

Charity, miffed, said, 'I think I do understand. I am eighteen, you know!'

'How could I forget?' laughed Sabina.

Cassandra told Charity some of her past 'falling tower' moment, but not everything. Nobody would learn all of it; not even Sabina had picked up on that. Cassandra had more of a reason to distrust men than mere infidelity.

As they ate, the conversation veered back to the hag of Dead Man's Wood. All the other diners had left. Sabina, taking advantage of their privacy, started to tell them all she knew.

'She's been seen by many people. Some tell of her and others do not for fear of ridicule.' Sabina clutched the polished blue crystal on her chest. 'During the witch hunts in the seventeenth century, she was accused of being a witch, but I think her only offence was the ability to cure, tell fortunes and have premonitions. Of course, that didn't sit well in society those days. She grew herbs, healed men and beasts, and was once called the Wise One. I suppose she was an easy target. Word got around that she must be in league with the devil and she was to be arrested for witchcraft.'

Charity cut in, 'Wow, that's weird.'

Sabina continued. 'She had always been a loner, living in isolation, but this is the strange bit.' She shuffled in her seat. 'Legend has it that she fled before they could arrest her. She just vanished, as though into thin air. Nobody knew where she had gone, she just disappeared as though she'd never existed.

'Some say it proved her witchery and that the devil helped her get away. Some even say she shape-shifted into a crow to avoid capture, and that every time you hear a crow it could be her and she will reside in Dead Man's Wood forever. It has also been said that sometimes she crosses into our time dimension and us into hers. People have been known to summon her in the woods for help with healing and spells.'

'That's weird,' whispered Cassandra again. 'I'm not sure I want to go back there.'

'Don't be afraid,' Sabina said in an upbeat tone. 'See it as something exciting, an adventure, if you will. You are on fate's journey now and this is only the beginning.'

Charity, intrigued, asked, 'Have you ever summoned her yourself for spells or healing, Mum?'

Sabina sighed heavily. 'No, I've never needed her services. It has never once crossed my mind to ask her for help. I don't think I've ever been that desperate.'

Finishing her lunch first, Sabina started to persuade Cassandra to come to the pub on Saturday evening. 'It's always a great atmosphere at weekends, especially if it stays warm. We can sit in the beer garden and listen to the music. It's a real laugh … a good atmosphere, isn't it, Charity?'

'Yes, weekends are great here,' Charity said mockingly. 'You don't need to go out of the village.'

Sabina continued, 'And it serves the best ale around, and Chardonnay, too.'

Charity agreed sarcastically. 'Yeah, the fun starts here!'

They were unaware that Saffron was still staring at them. She was leaning sideways against the back door of the kitchen in a hidden recess, watching them, her arms folded tightly across her chest.

12

Mark the builder, along with his sidekick Craig, was really getting stuck into the cottage. The electrician had placed his wires ready for the plaster, and the kitchen units had been ordered together with the bathroom suite, fixtures and fittings. They were now onto their second skip, and that was almost full.

The last few days had been unforgivingly hot and very long. Mark needed to speed up the schedule in order to get the job done. He hadn't had any other weird encounters and was keeping the radio on full blast, thinking it would keep the eerie spectre at bay. He also had the advantage of safety in numbers. The electrician had been working there, and the plumber was doing his bit. Every now and then, they would all stop for a break and a brew.

Delivery men turned up intermittently with further essential building materials and conversation. Every other word was 'mate'. The joiner, who was coming tomorrow, would no doubt contribute his own banter. As they all did their bit, the house was unfolding into a spectacular abode. Everything would come together into a seamless masterpiece worthy of Cassandra's praise. Well, that was the idea.

It was getting late and only Craig was with Mark, the others having retired for the day. Mark knew he had to tackle the back-kitchen recess but he'd been procrastinating as that was the place where the ghoul had manifested. The radio pulsed subtle tunes from the front room, muffled slightly with the distance and the closed door.

'Come here, Craig. Help me with this, will you, mate?' said Mark.

Craig strode toward him with his lanky swagger. 'What?'

They both looked into the recess. A light switch had been fitted and the bare wire was anchored temporarily to the wall, waiting to be plastered in. White light drowned the interior, a rare treat for such an ancient hermit's recess. The interior walls retained the uneven bulge of old plaster.

Mark said he needed help plastering the wire into position, then tomorrow a coat of white paint would brighten some of the exposed stone and old skin. The original stone-flagged floor continued into its hidden void and would look tidy enough, he thought.

He heard tapping coming from the wall, 'Tap, tap, tap.' He looked to Craig, who was busy with his finger in his ear, digging out some clogged wax and dirt.

'You what?' Craig said, examining the contents under his nail.

'Can you hear that?' said Mark.

'Hear what?' Craig wiped his finger on his shirt.

'Listen.' Mark took hold of Craig's shirt and yanked him closer to the wall.

'What?' said Craig. 'I can't hear anything.'

They listened intently to nothing but the muffled noise of the radio in the next room for at least twenty seconds. 'What am I listening for?' whispered Craig, a soppy grin on his face.

Mark was exasperated. 'Bloody hell! Nothing. We'll just do the bloody thing.' He was angry now at his growing fear of the ghoul making another entrance, but he carried on slapping the ready-made plaster into a hollow groove he'd made in the uneven surface. He anchored the wire and smoothed it as seamlessly as he could. The finished result was clumsy and rushed.

Craig carried on working in the front room, sweeping up the dusty mess the rubble had left. The fireplace had been opened up and had a brand-new, willow-green wood burner on a new stone hearth. A long, slightly curved oak lintel had been positioned as a mantel, its fresh wood a creamy white. They all complemented each other, enhancing the rustic feel of the exposed stone chimney breast. Oak beams, crooked and irregular, had been sanded down to their virgin glory to enhance the antiquated atmosphere.

Craig sang along to the music from the radio, happy it was nearly time to get off home. He didn't notice the drop in temperature, the wavy mist of an outline behind him, or the stare feeding from his energy. There was only one thing on his mind: what he would have for his tea.

The wispy fragile spectre tried to bristle the back of his neck with its unearthly tendrils, and even tried to enter his life-force aura, but he didn't respond. It stared at the back of his neck, confused. It wanted to be seen, to be acknowledged.

It was sending a message loud and clear: '*Get out, get out, get out, get out.*' It reached out ethereal strands again, screeching into his aura. '*Get out, get out, get out.*' Then it manifested into a hideous shape, its pinprick pupils piercing through a grey misty form, hunched over and grotesque. But its ectoplasmic form was wasted on Craig; he was too busy sweeping the floor and singing silently along, his lips mouthing the words to the tune on the radio.

As suddenly as it had come, the spectre receded into its default dimension of the tormented dead.

Mark came into the room, switched off the radio and made sure the light switches were off and the windows closed. 'Come on, lad,' he said. 'Let's go. Tomorrow's another day.' He shivered. 'It's nice and cool in here!'

As he turned leave, he saw a flash of movement across the open doorway in the hall. 'What was that?'

He went to investigate. Nothing but a fog of dust lingered in the hallway, but the kitchen door was wide open and he had closed it, ready to go out of the front door with Craig. Mark felt sickening fear roll in his stomach again, accompanied by a tingling sensation from the hairs on the back of his neck.

'Craig … Craig, come here a minute, will you?' he said, scratching his head.

'What's up?' Craig let the broom fall against the wall. Wiping his dirty hands down his shirt, he joined Mark at the doorway and peered into the hallway.

'Look! I just closed that door and now it is wide open again!'

Craig stepped past him and strode towards it. 'Maybe you didn't close it properly and it just swung open.' As he approached it, it suddenly slammed shut. The noise echoed through the dusty rafters of the empty house. The sudden bang was quickly absorbed by eerie silence.

They looked at each other in shock. Craig managed a groan. 'Um, what the hell?' He was scared now and felt his heartbeat pump up a notch.

Mark approached him cautiously, almost in slow motion, perturbed by his own clawing feelings of fear. He knew that the spectre was up to its tricks. Then Craig, his eyes wide, tried the handle again. He opened the door slowly to reveal the empty kitchen.

'Well, go on then. Have a look around.' Mark was down the hall.

Craig peered inside the room without moving his feet. 'No, I don't think there is anyone in here.'

'Go in and have a look around,' insisted Mark.

'You come with me!'

'Alright, we will go together.'

Mark, terrified and feeling quite cowardly, let Craig go first. The room held a waxy glow as the waning daylight teased shadows around the room. Noticing Craig's breath was now visible and the temperature had dropped dramatically, Mark said, 'Right then, there is nobody here. Come on, let's go.'

He thought he could hear a rustling movement coming from the recess where he had just re-plastered, so he pulled at Craig's arm. 'Come on, there's nobody here and I'm tired. Let's move it now!' He was anxious to get the hell out quickly before the spectre could prickle his hackles any more.

Craig obeyed gladly and closed the kitchen door behind himself. Mark locked up and they sped off in the transit van, both spooked but unwilling to share their thoughts and articulate what just happened.

Finally, Craig, confused, said, 'Wow, that's a spooky house.'

Mark glared at him with frightened eyes. 'Don't be so bloody stupid.'

They continued their journey home along the high street towards a mellow red sunset that was drenching the horizon.

13

The sunshine had settled comfortably into the afternoon, burning away any rogue clouds. Entering Dead Man's Wood was soothing, a welcome respite from the frazzling afternoon. Its lofty canopy of knitted branches giving a deep, earthy haze.

They followed the path, Charity leading the way until she came across the part of the path they had detoured from earlier. They couldn't smell burning or any indication that there ever had been; the air was sweet with woody aromas.

As they navigated the undergrowth in single file, Charity became confused. 'It should be here somewhere. We didn't go so deep into the woods,' she said, not knowing why she couldn't find the rickety house or the well-trodden clearing.

Cassandra scanned around her, looking for any indication of the little house and the hag.

Sabina, breathing deeply, was trying to tune into the zone they had found themselves in. 'I feel that it is close, very close now.' She let her senses guide the way through the rampant undergrowth, snapping branches and twigs to clear a path. She suddenly stopped, paused, and pointed downwards with her long pink fingernail. 'It is here! This is the spot.'

Charity and Cassandra looked about them, confused at her sudden revelation.

'What is? There is nothing here!' Charity looked at the dense greenery around them.

'Or should I say, it *was* here.' Sabina moved away tufts of foliage, ripping it up where she could. Bending down to look at the earth, she gave a triumphant sigh. 'Here, look!' She had exposed a stone flag.

They all joined in, pulling and scraping at the deep-rooted undergrowth. They didn't manage to reveal much, but what they did discover looked to have been the remnants of a floor. The hag's house? Most definitely.

'It's like I said before. You two must have witnessed a quantum moment where you slipped into her world. See – a simple explanation after all!' said Sabina.

Later that evening, they entered the Green Man and Sabina ordered a bottle of cold Chardonnay. Making their way out to the beer garden, they took a table next to a climbing honeysuckle. Its scent was pungent and sickly but delectable.

'Charity, you need to stay at the caravan with me until my cottage is fit to move into. Can you do that?' asked Cassandra, hoping she hadn't forgotten.

Charity placed her hand on her arm. 'Yes, of course I will.'

'Thank you so much. I feel a little more settled now.' Cassandra gulped down half her wine in one go, then felt her tummy flutter as Fenton Brooks entered the garden alone. There was half a pint left in his pint glass; he must have already been there. Her stomach was full of butterflies, and she felt annoyed again that he had so much of an effect on her.

He looked over to them. 'Hi, ladies, nice to see you.'

'Please come and join us. We need some male company, don't we, girls?' Sabina responded.

No, Cassandra thought, as he pulled up a chair next to her and smiled that warm smile.

'So, what have you been up to?' he asked shyly.

Sabina conducted the conversation and flirted with him with the confidence only an older woman could have. 'We've been watching you, haven't we, girls?'

Oh no! thought Cassandra. *What is she doing?*

'I am sure you have better things to watch,' he responded.

'We do,' said Charity, grinning at him.

'What do you think, Cassandra?' asked Sabina.

'What do I think about what?' She didn't want to be mixed up with him. She wanted all the feelings she had for him to go away. If she didn't engage with him, maybe he would be put out, get the message and go away? 'Yes, I definitely have better things to watch,' she said, her stare falling away from his eyes and onto her glass.

Sabina was perplexed, as though she wanted a good conversation between the four of them. She changed the subject. 'How's your father doing? Is he any better?' She looked genuinely concerned.

'Not too bad. Some days are more difficult than others, but we manage and the carer comes to the farm twice a day to see to his needs. I wish I could look after him full time, but,' he smiled showing his strong white teeth, 'I have to work. Needs must and all that.'

His gaze fell onto Cassandra. She wondered what was wrong with his father. A wave of compassion consumed her and with slight trepidation she enquired further, her eyes conveying more than she could say. 'Fenton, I am so sorry. Is your father not well?'

'He has liver cancer. His pain is under control but it's terminal. I'm trying to keep him home for as long as possible. It's what he wants. He was born on the farm and it has been his whole life. He says he wants to die there on his own hallowed ground, not in a hospital in town – and I don't blame him. The farm has been in the family for generations. I don't think he ever got over the death of my mother about six years ago. She had cancer too.' He looked down at his pint as though the memories were too difficult to articulate.

Cassandra did not know what to say. She'd had no idea he was going through so much. She realised that in only a few seconds she had totally changed her mind about him. He must be extremely vulnerable at the moment and no doubt in need of some respite from his cruel situation.

She couldn't prevent the words spilling from her mouth. 'If ever you need anything just let me know,' she said. She realised how insincere it sounded, as though she were being polite, but she meant it. 'Anything at all I can do to help, please don't hesitate.'

Sabina cut in. 'Yes, that goes for all of us, Fenton.'

'Yes, me too,' Charity said.

The air was thick with emotion. Sabina stood up briskly, fending off the distressing paralysis the conversation had triggered, and said, 'Right, I'm going to the bar for another bottle. I'll get you another pint, Fenton.'

Charity shouted after her, 'I'll help you with the drinks.' She followed her mother, leaving Cassandra and Fenton alone.

The atmosphere was taut and Cassandra didn't know what to say. She couldn't change the conversation to a lighter tone without sounding rude. Then Fenton smiled and said, 'Let's talk about something nicer.'

Cassandra allowed herself a smile too and started to relax. The high temperature outside was being diluted sporadically with a wash of lukewarm breeze that stroked their hair and brushed against their bare arms, giving some relief from the intense heat.

Then Fenton asked her a question she would rather not have answered in full. 'What brought you to this village of all places?'

She told him just enough, but not all of it. 'I needed a change, I suppose, a fresh start...' She laughed. 'A new adventure!'

'In Whalley Dell?' he quizzed cheekily.

'It's as good a place as any. I needed a slower pace, a more sedate rhythm to chill out my life a little. I know I've taken on a challenge with the cottage but, believe me, once it is finished it will be a palace.'

'Cassandra, I know it will be, I admire your courage for taking on such a task.'

She loved it when he said her name. His voice was deep but kind, with a sultry warmth.

'Here we are.' Sabina was back, placing his fresh pint in front of him. Charity was behind her, holding a silver ice bucket with the white wine inside.

They sat in happy conversation for at least twenty minutes. Cassandra was relaxing into the pleasure it brought but then, to her dismay, she saw Saffron's brother, ginger-haired Sam, approaching.

'Hi, Fenton, I'm glad I've seen you. Do you want to join us inside? The match has started.' Sam's freckled skin was red with the summer's onslaught.

Fenton could only say, 'Yes, why not?' As he stood up to leave, he thanked Sabina for the drink and glanced apologetically at Cassandra.

Sabina said, 'Go and enjoy yourself, Fenton. We will be here a while, won't we, girls?'

Cassandra felt she needed to come up for air. He had such a hypnotic effect on her.

'See you later, Fenton,' she said, her eyes locking with his.

70

'I do hope so,' he managed, then strode away to join his buddies in the bar.

She didn't take her eyes from him until he disappeared, his broad shoulders dissolving into the greedy darkness inside.

'See, he is nice, isn't he?' said Sabina, watching her watching Fenton.

Cassandra allowed herself a smile of acknowledgement. 'Yes, he is.'

'Wow, you've changed your tune,' laughed Charity, making Cassandra realise how wrong it had been to pre-judge him, just like her ex-fiancé but in the opposite way. She would be more mindful in future and not allow any pre-conceived ideas to influence her again. Well, she'd try anyway.

14

Later, as they left the Green Man, intermittent roars and cheers from the pub washed into the high street. No doubt the match had turned out to be a good one.

'Come on,' said Sabina, 'we'll leave Fenton to enjoy himself. I think he needs it.'

Following the main road, they veered off into the meadow, allowing the dusty path to take them to the star-dazzled caravan. An ochre moon enhanced the sparkles in the shimmering paint, making it look ethereal in the lunar glow.

Cassandra ran in front, scaled the wooden steps and unlocked the door. She switched on a lamp, its illumination sending pale light through the tiny windows and open doorway. 'I'll put the kettle on,' she shouted, retrieving clean cups and a pack of biscuits from the kitchen cupboard.

They sat around the little table on cushioned chairs. The silence outside allowed the subtle hum of nature to dominate and strum eerily through the grasses and flowers in the meadow.

Sabina asked Cassandra, 'How are you finding it here? Do you like it?'

'Yes,' she said. 'I love it, apart from the weirdo staring at me from the woods the other day. And I'm a bit apprehensive about moving back into the cottage with the ghostly sitting tenant.'

'Don't worry,' said Sabina. 'We'll sort it out. We're used to things like that. If I can't send it on its way, I know many who can.'

'It's such a spooky place. I wasn't anticipating anything like this.'

'But I'm staying with you now,' chirped Charity. 'I'll get my things in a minute.'

'Go and get them now,' Sabina said, 'before it gets too late.'

Charity went outside and navigated the path, the warmth of the night and the light of the moon accompanying her. Suddenly she let out a cry. It travelled over the meadow and into the open door and windows of the caravan. 'Mum, come here! What is this?'

Sabina and Cassandra ran outside to the back garden of the house where they found Charity, with her hand over her mouth, looking at something that had been nailed to the wooden garden gate. The yellow moon shone on it like a spotlight, revealing a freakish display.

There were three effigies: one of Sabina, one of Charity and the other of Cassandra. Fashioned from clumsy stitched hessian, their faces had been deformed to represent crude gargoyles. They had a macabre similarity to each of the women and it was evident the artist had spent quite a time getting their likenesses just right.

Sabina's had long burgundy hair made from coarse wool; Charity's had long brown string for hair, and Cassandra's had very short white string. They were around six inches in length, and all three had been hanged. Thick string was intricately fashioned into nooses, looped over their heads and pulled tight at the neck.

Cassandra felt suddenly nauseous and retreated slowly from them. 'What is this, Sabina?' she asked. 'Why would anyone do this? It's sick and twisted.'

Sabina sighed. 'You would think people had better things to do with their time.'

'Obviously somebody out there doesn't like us.' Charity shivered at the macabre sight.

'Someone is trying to frighten us, that's all. But we will not let the fear in.' Sabina tried to pull the dolls from the gate, but the string had been wrapped tightly and knotted around three separate nails to form their makeshift gallows. The hideous faces had been intricately painted with pin-point black eyes and creepy red smiles.

'Get the big scissors in the kitchen drawer, Charity,' Sabina said. When Charity returned, she levered the nails from the gate. The wood split slightly as she released them, and the dolls fell to the ground in a heap.

'What do we do with them now?' asked Cassandra, her shock aggravating her nausea.

'We need a creamy yellow candle.' Sabina went into the kitchen to get one and some matches. Returning to the caravan, carrying the hideous dolls with her, she placed them on the floor. Then she asked, 'What do you see in these dolls?'

Charity answered first. 'They are supposed to represent us, aren't they? And whoever put them there want us dead, maybe humiliated first.'

'That's right, Charity. Cassandra, what do you see?'

Cassandra's voice was firm and defiant. 'I see the product of someone's sick, twisted mind. What kind of lunatic would do this, and why?'

Sabina took several deep breaths and her voice was determined and instructional, like a teacher in a classroom. 'The intention of the perpetrator is to scare us, to frighten us into thinking they are more powerful than we are. I have come across this so many times in the past and the key is to see it for what it is – a sad little prank by a sad little person. We must not entertain any fears it may provoke. We are more powerful than this silly...' she paused looking for the right word '...buffoonery, and dismiss it for what it is. The more we have fearful thoughts, the more fuel is added to the fire. They are nothing but a trio of silly little dolls and they have no control over us. They mean nothing to us whatsoever.'

She opened one of the drawers in the tiny kitchen and took out something which looked like a soft bundle of rags. 'This is dried sage and it cleanses negative energy.'

She struck a match. Its bright spark illuminated their baffled faces before settling into a soft silent flame, its smooth glow the colour of egg yolk. She set fire to one end of the long bundle, giving it life, then shook away the flame to reveal a crimson studded glow. 'The Native American Indians use this technique in cleansing rituals – and it works.'

The interior of the caravan filled with spirals of powdery grey smoke. The aroma was sweet yet earthy and musky. As she moved it around, it stroked the air in slow motion, wrapping long tendrils around everything as though an ethereal intelligence were steering it.

Sabina picked up each doll in turn, letting the curls encase them, then she asked the Divine to cleanse and eradicate any evil intent within each doll, thus rendering them harmless.

Taking the cream-coloured candle and placing it in a glass holder, she lit it carefully. Nobody made a sound, as if a new energy were beginning to pulsate into the caravan that nobody wanted to spoil.

Spreading the dolls into a row on the hard floor, Sabina chanted, 'I have no fear of these before me. I cast any residual hateful energy into the candle. Now concentrate on the dancing flame,' she said, as it spiked higher and higher into the air.

Cassandra was amazed that such a small candle could produce such a tall flame.

Continuing with intense concentration, Sabina said, 'Any pain or fear is now transferred into the flame to cleanse it away once and for all. Cassandra, leave the candle to burn through the night and don't let the flame go out before it has burnt all the way to the bottom.'

'Okay, no pressure then. What if it goes out?' asked Cassandra, feeling overwhelmed.

'It won't,' said Sabina.

Cassandra had a disturbing thought she had to share. 'Was it the ghostly weirdo in the woods the other day?'

'No, I don't think so. My intuition leads me to someone, though. We will find out who this was.' Sabina glared. 'I am sure that if we give them enough rope, they will hang themselves.'

She left Cassandra and Charity in the caravan for the night and made her way back to the house. They were now alone in bed with the lamps off. It was eerily quiet; the only light came from the dancing candle flame as it stretched its long, flickering tongue into the caravan, licking the walls with moving shadows.

15

Just before dawn, Saffron awoke at the farmhouse. A cooling breeze was filtering through her open window. She stepped across the bare floorboards of her bedroom and down the corridor to her dated, avocado-coloured bathroom, circa 1970. Showering over the bath, she soaped herself ready to brave the morning ahead.

Quickly scrubbing her teeth and cleansing her face and neck, she made herself presentable for the day with a subtle dusting of makeup and a waxy, coral-coloured lipstick. She pulled a long pink-and-red hippy-style dress over her head, struggling slightly as she squeezed it over her shapely breasts. A large oval moonstone crystal, the colour of white mist, dangled from a long silver chain adorning her cleavage.

She looked out from her bedroom window at Dead Man's Wood in the distance. Strands of white-and-gold sunlight teased the horizon. Holding the gemstone in her hand, she closed her eyes and muttered an indecipherable incantation that only she knew. Although she was hungry, she would forego breakfast; her body had to be pure for this sacred mission.

The day was not yet warm, so she pulled on a short, buff-coloured cardigan. Anchoring her multi-coloured tote bag over her shoulder, she made her way along the path to Dead Man's Wood. The bag held a gift for the host she was to meet.

A chorus of birdsong accompanied her, its melody a shrill and erratic riot of noise. She entered into the mouth-like void of the wood and, like walking into a gothic building, the energy suddenly changed. It always did at dawn, beckoning and opening a pocket of otherworldliness and magic.

Pacing a well-worn path, she paused as sunlight glinted through the canopy of branches, breathing life into them. A shrill cry from a crow drowned out the birdsong, then there was a noise, a rustling, behind her. Was there another presence in this magical wooded environment?

Suddenly the whole atmosphere seemed to be breathing, energy speeding up behind her and gaining momentum. A voice, sharp and bossy, made her spin around. Standing before her was the hag of Dead Man's Wood.

'I thought it be you,' she said. 'What is it now?' Her piercing blue eyes contrasted with her dirty face. She stared at Saffron as though she knew exactly what she wanted. 'What did I tell ye before? You don't need me,' she said. 'Mind your own business.'

'But I have a problem.'

'It be a man?'

'Yes.'

The hag stayed silent for a while, all the time glaring at Saffron. Finally she said, 'Ah, I see there's another maid has notions about him. Am I right?'

'Yes, you are. What can I do?' asked Saffron desperately.

'You know the rules. I ask ye three questions, then you can ask me three. Ye have got me a gift?' She wiped her bony hand against her dirt-creased mouth.

'Yes, of course.' Saffron held the bag aloft and took out a bottle of red wine. She placed it on the ground between them.

The hag spat her first question at Saffron. 'Do ye think ye can change the fates?'

Saffron looked hesitant, her eyes pleading for the right answer. 'Yes, I think I can.' Her answer hung uncomfortably in the air.

The hag responded sharply, 'No, ye cannot – unless ye want to be in bed with the devil.' Then came her second question: 'What is his name?'

'Fenton ... Fenton Brooks,' said Saffron, sheepishly.

'Ahh.' The hag began to cackle to herself. Her open mouth was nothing but a shiny black hole with splinters of rusty decaying bone inside. She asked her next question, 'And pray, what be her name?'

'Cassandra ... I don't know her last name. She's new to the village and is living in the caravan in the meadow.'

'Ah, yes,' said the hag. 'She be tall and fair with eyes like golden silk.' Bending down, she picked up two fallen twigs and held them tightly, one in each hand. 'You may ask your three questions now, lass.'

Saffron searched the ground, wondering how to word her first question. 'How can I make him mine and not hers?'

The hag answered slowly, almost menacingly. 'Like I told ye before, ye cannot mess with the fates. Ye can do nothing but hope and wait. If it is meant by the fates, it will be.'

Saffron stayed silent, not wanting to accept the answer. Then, with a wave of boldness, she asked her second question. 'What can I do? There must be something to increase my chances?'

'Nothing – unless ye want to dance with the devil, lass.' The hag retrieved her bottle of wine from the ground and prepared to walk away.

'Stop,' said Saffron. 'You promised me three questions and this is my third. What must I do?'

'Ye know what to do. Ye must get rid of her – but that is not my advice, lass, it is my answer. Maybe try the black salt. If it is meant, she will go.'

Suddenly a dark cloud shrouded the fledgling light and a whirling wind whipped up around them. As her clothes flapped about, the hag said, 'In these woods ye find many things, but beware of what they bring. Not all plants bring good from seed. Some are bad, so take good heed.'

Then she was gone, disappearing as though she'd never been there, leaving Saffron alone in the woods again with nothing but her answer and the dawn sunlight twinkling against the canopy of trees. She sat there alone and, as the dawn chorus subsided, she was embraced by a hypnotic silence. Then she noticed the time.

Two hours had passed. Knowing the café opened at 7.30, Saffron decided to satisfy her growling hunger by having breakfast on the high street. She knew what to do now. She was certain the hag was suggesting a banishment spell, and if that didn't work maybe hemlock.

She felt the energy had shifted from stalemate to all systems go. Fuelled by her elation, she trudged across the edge of the meadow, looking back every now and again to see if anyone had seen her. Although she felt a twinge of guilt, it was overridden by her desperation. What else could she do? She had to get rid of Cassandra, didn't she?

16

Cassandra awoke early to a musty smell and a burnt-out candle. She noticed it had burnt down all the way and felt relieved it hadn't extinguished prematurely during the night. She moved the dolls with her foot to the corner of the caravan; although rendered harmless now, she didn't want to touch them.

Realising a creeping fear was trying to get hold of her, she repeated the words Sabina had chanted last night: 'I have no fear of these before me.' As her mood lightened, she put on the kettle to boil and took some coffee from the cupboard.

Charity came up behind her rubbing her eyes. 'I would love a coffee. Any croissants left?'

'Yes. Sit down, I'll get them.'

As Cassandra looked out from the small window in front of her, she noticed the long grasses and flowers moving with the breeze, rippling and simmering with life. Something caught her eye; in the distance, she saw what looked like Saffron running along the outskirts of the meadow.

It had only just gone 7.15am – where was she going at such a time, or where was she coming from? She was half-running, then every few seconds she looked behind her into Dead Man's Wood as though she were fleeing from something or someone.

Cassandra peered towards the black wood but saw nothing but its dense twisting mass, such a contrast to the flamboyant meadow. Maybe she could go and ask Saffron, but the girl was far away now, just a moving blur on the horizon heading towards the high street. Could she catch her up? She hoped so – she wanted to make sure they were still friends. Saffron snubbing her at the pub the other day had made her think otherwise.

Keen to catch up with her before she entered the high street, Cassandra hugged her flimsy dressing gown around her and ran down the wooden steps. She did not take the curving path but a short cut and ran through the lush flowers in hot pursuit. The early morning dew had not yet been dried by the fledgling sunshine, and cool moisture oozed, almost slimy against her legs, saturating her gown.

'Saffron! Saffron!' shouted Cassandra as loud as she could, but her cries would not carry across such a distance. It was useless. She saw Saffron enter the high street, a dot in the distance now disappearing around the corner.

Wading back through the grasses, her slippers soggy and her legs drenched, she climbed back into the caravan to see Charity finishing off the coffee.

'What was that?' Charity asked. 'I wondered where you'd gone!'

'Oh, nothing. I thought I saw Saffron in the distance. She seemed to be running away. I thought I could get her attention but she was too far away.'

Intrigued, Charity said, 'Really? Why would Saffron be out at this time? And why would she be running?'

Cassandra went onto the porch to scan the horizon, her hand shielding her eyes from the early sunshine. 'Maybe she will be at the Green Man tonight. We'll quiz her then.'

After breakfast, Charity went to open up her mum's shop, leaving Cassandra alone with her thoughts. She was thinking about the renovations at her cottage and was keen to see what progress had been made, if any. Could it be as bad as the last time she'd seen it? She had told Mark she would pop round at about two o'clock and was excited to see its ongoing transformation.

Gazing out from the porch into the rainbow blanket of wild flowers, her attention was drawn by the shrill squawk of a black crow bobbing its heavy body up and down on a nearby bush. Its small darting eyes were investigating the space around it, and she wondered if it was the shapeshifting hag of Dead Man's Wood.

17

Nearly a full week had passed since the renovations had begun on Cassandra's cottage, and Mark wasn't so spooked anymore. Although the radio was on full blast, hopefully shooing away the spectre, the other tradesmen were adding their disturbance to the mix, and there was commotion inside and outside. Mark knew this particular ghost was a bully and preferred one-on-one confrontation; although the noise was sometimes deafening, he was pacified by the notion of safety in numbers.

Dave the joiner had fitted the new kitchen units and worktop, and started to tackle the creaky oak staircase, hammering and mending its broken bones. Some of the treads had to be replaced but it was sound enough, free of woodworm and would, in his opinion, 'endow its master with another hundred years of service'.

Mark thought it was a macabre structure, but Cassandra wanted to retain as much of the original character of the cottage as possible, and that included the staircase. She was coming around this afternoon to inspect the renovations. Feeling quite proud of himself, he couldn't wait to show her all the progress made. Another week and she'd probably be moving in.

He chatted to the plumber, who was finishing off connecting the glossy white Belfast sink under the kitchen window; it looked striking against the black granite worktop. The cottage was slowly coming together like an intricate jigsaw puzzle. There was an atmosphere of style and vitality in the kitchen now, with French-grey shaker units replacing the archaic flimsy carcasses.

In just a week, the house seemed to have changed its personality and acquired a jovial feel. The agreeable scent of fresh paint filled the voids of neglect. He knew Cassandra would be pleased.

***

'Hello, hello…?' Cassandra squeezed past one of the workmen to announce her presence amid the chaos, clatter and hammering. At least she was smiling this time as she walked past the staircase and into the kitchen.

'Wow, this is wonderful. What a difference.' She moved around slowly, running her hand along the worktop and relishing its smooth texture. Its surface still held a sheath of gritty dust but it would look awesome when it was cleaned and polished.

She opened cupboards and drawers; they glided effortlessly, displaying quality and high-class workmanship. Appliances had been built in, including a dishwasher, fridge-freezer, oven and gas hob. There was even a stylish wine cooler. Cassandra's beaming smile was infectious, and Mark couldn't stop a proud smile from forming on his dirty, sweaty face.

'Your washer-dryer is in the alcove over here,' he said, pointing to the recess where the ghost had played its tricks. 'I suppose it is your utility room, but it's a very small one.' Flicking on the light switch he illuminated the space.

A wall-to-ceiling double pantry door had been fashioned to hide everything, painted in French grey to match the rest of the room. The thick walls had been re-plastered and washed with white emulsion. The whole room seemed to glow and shout delight at its own existence. All she needed was a decent ceiling light and a blind for the kitchen window, then it would be complete. Mark was glad the new wooden stable door was open to allow a sun-blushed scent of greenery to enter from the rear garden.

'I love it,' she said smiling, then went to look around the rest of the house.

Dave the joiner was finishing his work for the day. He had an appointment; looking at his watch he said, 'Right, that's me for the day, Mark. I'll be back in the morning. See you, mate.'

Reaching for his tools, he went out into the dazzling two o'clock sunshine. He left the front door open and a dry stream of air gently trespassed along the hallway, gently dispersing arid dust into a flurry, coaxing a mini-tornado to strum against the structure of the staircase. Weaving through its joints, it caused one of the steps to relinquish one of its secrets.

Mark looked at the dust cascading into the hallway and decided to close the front door. As he walked back, he noticed something on one of the treads, fluttering at the edges as though desperate to be acknowledged. From a distance, it looked to be a stained envelope.

He gently lifted the dusty item and turned it over. It was a Christmas card, and an old one at that. It displayed a colourful drawing of a red-and-white toadstool with windows and a door. Yellow light shone from its windows into festive, snow-dappled surroundings. A baby deer stood looking in through the window at a cheeky elf that was looking out.

He tried to open it but its time-blistered edges had curled up and stuck the card shut.

'Hey, Cassandra look at this,' he said. 'I found it on the staircase.'

She was surveying the cosy living room, admiring the oak mantle and wood burner in the fire place. 'What's this?' she asked, as he handed her the card.

'I found it on the stairs. It must have escaped from somewhere when the wind blew in.'

She took it and teased its rolled-up edges flat, trying to open it to reveal its message. The card was stubborn and resisted, making a cracking sound as she gently pulled it open. Hesitantly, it relinquished its underbelly to the twenty-first century. Elegant time-faded scroll imparted a message inside:

Happy Christmas,
Flo, Agnes and Lilly
With love Mary xxx

18

After meeting at Sabina's cottage, the three of them set off to the Green Man pub for some escape from the week's unpredictable temperament. The air smelt celestial as they sauntered along the path through the meadow, their hands stroking the tall flowers and grasses along the way.

As they entered the high street, they heard muffled rhythmic melodies coming from inside the fortress-like ale house. The music was indecipherable, shielded by the thick stone walls, but once inside it became recognisable. There was a heady odour of ale and food, and they could almost taste its potency as they inhaled.

They made their way to the bar and melted into the welcoming atmosphere. The music bounced around the crowded interior, escaping into the beer garden from the open doors at the back.

Saffron was busy behind the bar serving customers, and Frank the landlord was effortlessly pulling at a pump, pooling lager into a pint glass. He acknowledged them with a wink and a smile.

Sabina ordered two bottles of Chardonnay. 'Where you sitting, love? I'll bring them to you,' said Frank.

'Out the back, Frank.' She gestured towards the beer garden.

They settled into chairs under a solid oak tree next to the carved wooden statue of the Green Man, its impish face glaring at them curiously. A handful of young women danced barefoot on the grassy spaces between the tables, no doubt animated by the flowing alcohol.

Cassandra began to relax, then she saw Saffron bringing over the wine and glasses, nudging and dodging through customers along the way. She wasn't smiling, and Cassandra knew there was something bothering her. She followed the girl back into the pub and said, 'Is anything wrong?'

Saffron spun around in surprise, then demanded, 'What do you mean?'

'Have I done something to upset you?'

Saffron looked her up and down. 'I am working,' she said, then walked away.

Snubbed again by Saffron, Cassandra decided to go to the ladies' toilet. Opening the squeaky door, she found herself in an unusually cold room with cubicles on one side and two sinks on the other under a mirrored wall. Enjoying the welcome respite from the heat of the day, she placed her wrists under the cold tap to cool herself down.

A lady came out from one of the cubicles and stood directly behind her, not moving an inch. 'Isn't that sink working?' asked Cassandra. She tried the other tap, which worked perfectly.

'I'm not here for that. I'm here get some peace.' The young woman was now standing beside her and looking at her reflection in the mirror. She was short and frail, with untended hair tied into a knot at the back. Strands had escaped onto her pasty face, and her eyes were a washed-out blue, pooled with tears. Although she was wearing a long, retro-style dress, she looked dishevelled and not at all like someone who had groomed themselves for a night out. She had a pitiful look about her, a kind of miserable desperation.

The young woman stared at Cassandra's reflection in the mirror and tried to smile, to crease her dehydrated lips. 'I had better go now.' She turned to leave, her long dress scraping the floor as she carried herself out of the room, not by the door but into the wall next to the door.

Cassandra, gasping in horror, grabbed the door and pulled it towards her. It opened up to the familiar world of banter, music and warmth. Her face flushed with shock, she returned to Sabina and Charity, her mind in a confused haze.

Sabina, seeing her troubled face, stood up. 'Are you alright?' she asked. 'I saw you talk to Saffron. Has she upset you?'

Cassandra sat down, poured herself a full glass of wine and gulped nearly all of it down in one go. 'God, I needed that,' she said, trying to compose herself.

Sabina and Charity stared at her, waiting for her to speak.

'I've just seen a bloody ghost.'

Annoyingly, Sabina sighed. 'Oh, is that all? I thought Saffron had upset you.'

Cassandra tried not to glare. 'What do you mean, is that all? I'm a nervous wreck.'

'I did tell you to prepare yourself for opening up to the spirit. You are sensitive now. Who did you see? Was it a young woman?'

'What did she look like?' added Charity.

Cassandra took some deep breaths. 'She was small and skinny, with her hair tied back. She was wearing a long dress... I thought it was a real person until she walked straight through the toilet wall.'

'Wow!' said Charity. 'It was probably Lizzy. She's been seen a few times, but she's never shown herself to me.'

Sabina explained, 'Lizzy was the scullery maid here in the 1700s. They say she died after being beaten up by her father. Her father found out she was pregnant, barged into the Green Man and beat the life out of her – and, of course, her baby.'

'My God, that's horrible.' Cassandra gulped more of her wine.

'It is, and it's quite sad because she should be moved on. She's earthbound, trapped as a ghost in this dimension. She needs peace.'

'That's what she said to me,' said Cassandra. 'She said, "I need some peace." She must be in torment.'

'I've asked Frank if I can move her on, but he won't let me. He says it is good for business having a resident ghost.' Sabina sighed.

'Could you not move her on without him knowing?'

'I wouldn't dare – his pub, his property and his ghost.' She shrugged her shoulders.

'Surely there must be something we can do to help her cross into the light,' pressed Cassandra, still a bit shaky.

'We need his permission first.'

The music was a welcome respite from the uncomfortable energy of Lizzy's ghost. In a strange sort of way, Cassandra felt she was getting used to all the creepy goings-on in the village.

Charity raised her glass in a toast. 'Welcome to Whalley Dell, the ghost capital of the world.' All three of them laughed, their humour melting away the strange and macabre elements.

'Tell you what,' said Sabina, 'I'll ask him again if we can come in and investigate one evening after closing time. He might go for that.'

'That would be interesting. Ask him if we can stay after closing tonight.'

'I suppose I can only try.' Sabina had a curious glint in her green eyes.

They watched the pub garden fill up with more customers, oblivious to the fact that a ghost prowled among them. Later, when dusk settled and the outdoor lights illuminated their surroundings, Fenton Brooks strolled out from the pub with Sam and Jo. They sat nearby, pints in hand, relaxing into the laid-back atmosphere and watching the young women dancing. Fenton glanced Cassandra's way and acknowledged her with a wave of his hand. He smiled and she smiled back, but he didn't come over.

Cassandra saw Saffron approach him, her wide smile revealing her elation. She watched them talk and laugh for at least a minute and was unprepared for the wash of jealousy that consumed her. She felt disappointed at them flirting together – but also annoyed that she felt that way.

Frank agreed for them to stay after last orders to have a look round the pub whilst it was empty. The last of the stragglers reluctantly left about 11.15pm, their laughing banter echoing up the street as they made their way home.

Fenton had left early, but Saffron was still working behind the bar. All was quiet, yet the energy of the night's merriment still pervaded the atmosphere.

After Saffron had left for home, Frank finished loading the glasses, their shrill clanking slicing through the mugginess inside. 'Right, I'll leave you to it,' he said. Then he smiled. 'Let me know what you find.'

'You'll be the first to know, don't worry,' said Sabina.

He left them in semi-darkness and silence.

'Right, let's begin.' Sabina took Cassandra and Charity's hands and they formed a circle. 'I ask that we be totally protected by the pure white light of the Christ, through which nothing negative can penetrate. Focus on a cleansing, spiritual, platinum-

and-white energy swirling into the room. Allow it in, feel it all around us. We are now protected.'

She turned to Cassandra. 'Ask her if she will show herself. You seem to have a connection with her.'

Cassandra whispered into the shadows, 'Please come forward, Lizzy. We want to help you.' Nothing happened, so she tried again. Again nothing.

Then something moved behind the bar; there was a rattle of glasses and a bang, something falling onto the floor.

'Is that you, Lizzy?' Cassandra asked. 'Please show yourself to me if you can, like you did earlier today. We want to help you.'

A piercing cry split the air. The shadowy form of Lizzy emerged, pale, with frosty, weeping eyes staring anxiously into the space between them. She seemed to communicate a painful despair deeper than mere words could convey.

Cassandra continued, 'We want to help you. Lizzy. Why are you still here? You should be with the light, away from this earthly dimension. What is wrong?'

'I can't find him. I keep looking, but he is not here,' the spectre answered.

'Find who, Lizzy? Who can't you find?' asked Sabina.

'Thomas, my man. He said he wouldn't let anything bad happen and that we would be married, but I can't find him and my dad is going to kill me. He's coming now.' She was shaking hysterically, pointing her frail finger into the shadows at a grotesque heap on the floor behind them.

They turned around to see a wooden bucket tipped over on its side. Next to it lay the unrecognizable form of a young woman with a bruised and swollen face. An open split on the lip revealed dislodged teeth in a hideous smile. Blood and spilt water was pooling all around her.

Sabina said, 'Don't break the circle. Breathe in the light. I call upon the angels of heaven to take you to the light. Don't be afraid. I feel them now.'

A golden energy portal opened up like a tunnel. Seeing the opportunity, Cassandra, shouted, 'Go, Lizzy! Go now into the light! Can you see it, feel its pull? It will take you to Thomas and your loved ones on the other side. Go now.'

There was a sudden implosion of energy and, in the blink of an eye, Lizzy had gone. The atmosphere lifted and changed from a cold frantic desperation to a warm glow.

'Did you feel that sudden shift when she went?' Cassandra asked. 'It was so quick! I can't believe we just did that.'

'This is your first spirit rescue. Maybe the first of many,' said Sabina. 'Well done both of you.'

They sat down, relishing the lighter energy the divine had gifted.

'What do we say to Frank now she's gone? He might not be too happy,' asked Charity, flushed from the experience.

'We will tell him that we had an encounter with her, and that his pub was and is haunted by Lizzy. He won't know any different,' whispered Sabina.

The other ghosts did not show themselves that night. They had taken up residence in many of the rooms over the centuries, and each had their own story to tell.

19

The following night, keen to embrace their newfound friendship, Cassandra met up with Sabina and Charity at the caravan about 7.30pm. They went across the meadow to the high street for another evening at the Green Man. Feeling excited as she approached, Cassandra heard invigorating music spilling into the street from the beer garden round the back.

A silent breeze stroked the air and the pub sign swung smoothly, its frail squeak unable to compete with the loud music and banter pulsating behind it.

Entering the beer garden, they were transported into a dimension of carefree frivolity and celebration. The wooden carving of the Green Man was illuminated, emphasising its dominance of the garden, which was already filling up with keen revellers. Cassandra's stomach somersaulted at the thought of Fenton being there.

'Come on, let's find a seat.' Sabina guided them towards the familiar mature oak tree. Its slow-moving branches, lush and welcoming, were sheltering an empty table and chairs.

'I'll get the wine, you two save this table.' Sabina strolled across the lawn into the pub doorway, smiling in greeting to people she knew along the way.

Cassandra was happy that she had a good view of everyone coming and going; if Fenton were here, she would find him easily.

Then she saw him; Sabina was bringing the wine and glasses over, and Fenton was helping her. Their eyes met and Cassandra, feeling butterflies all over again, stood up to greet him. 'It's lovely to see you, Fenton. Have you been here long?'

'Only about twenty minutes. I was just chatting to the lads inside.' He looked around. 'It's really getting going now, isn't it?'

People were laughing and dancing barefoot on the grass, fuelled by the flowing alcohol and a peculiar desire to dance around the Green Man carving, Nature's fertility deity.

Later, when Sabina went to get more drinks from the bar, Charity strode behind her to help, leaving Cassandra alone with Fenton.

She saw a still figure staring at them from the dance floor and realised it was Saffron. People were rubbing shoulders with her, some walking past and trying to talk to her, but she didn't seem to notice them. She looked as though she were in a daze. Cassandra waved, trying to get her attention, but Saffron didn't respond.

Sabina and Charity returned from the bar and sat down. 'Is that Saffron over there?' asked Sabina, noticing her strange demeanour.

'It is. I'll invite her over.' Cassandra waved again but Saffron still snubbed her.

Cassandra looked at Sabina. 'Did you see that?'

Sabina nodded. 'Yes, I did. What's up with her?'

Fenton stood up and tried to get Saffron's attention. She immediately acknowledged him with a wide smile, walked eagerly towards him and flung her arms wide to give him a welcoming hug. Then she kissed him on the cheek.

Cassandra received Saffron's unspoken message loud and clear: 'He's mine!' She watched as Saffron and Fenton walked into the pub together.

They had both snubbed her, but her mood lifted when they returned. Saffron was now holding a large glass of red wine between her glossy lobster-coloured fingernails and had a smug smile on her face.

The music was animating everyone, and the sun was holding court as it reluctantly descended into the horizon and flooded the sky with its fiery glow. Customers mingled, drinking and chattering. The air was alive, gossip and laughter blending with throbbing music. Now and then, there was a wisp of cool breeze, but only fleetingly, as though the crowded atmosphere were bullying it away.

Dusk was descending. Strings of fairy lights decorated the trees and trellises, ready to take over after the sun retired.

Saffron placed her glass on the table and pulled Fenton towards the dance floor. 'No, no,' he protested, pulling back.

'Oh, come on, Fenton. Dance with me.' Her eyes were glassy and her smile garish with too much red lipstick.

Reluctantly, he gave in. She held onto his shoulders, forcing his hands onto her waist, moving sensuously to the music. Fenton didn't seem to be enjoying it, and he turned to look apologetically at Cassandra.

Cassandra instinctively knew what Saffron was up to and almost enjoyed his embarrassment. She was struggling not to laugh but didn't want to upset him, so she sat there with her glass of cold Chardonnay watching the entertainment they had gifted her – albeit with a twinge of guilt for being so amused.

20

Cassandra looked wonderful, but Saffron did not see her as she was. She did not see that Cassandra was shapely, with flawless skin, sun-bleached hair and natural beauty. To Saffron, Cassandra was a whore on heat who was after her man – but she was going to put things straight, starting tonight.

Saffron loved the feel of Fenton's strong hands around her waist and was elated that he was now dancing with her. She hoped Cassandra would get the message.

The party was in full swing, with everyone milling around, anesthetised with alcohol, wild abandon and lost inhibitions. Cassandra's kind white smile aggravated her; Saffron managed to smile back, but only to abate any suspicion of her evil intentions.

The night continued in a frenzy of merriment, then suddenly the music changed from seductive to a more energetic beat. Fenton immediately left Saffron alone on the dance floor, as though eager to get back to Cassandra. Her plan had backfired.

Saffron, shocked and abandoned, decided to mingle amongst the partygoers away from Cassandra and her clan. She did not want to make polite conversation with them. She couldn't wait to do her dirty deed. She watched them, her deep eyes glinting in the fading sunset. She had a few more glasses of red wine then blended into the shadows, watching from afar.

It was now 10.30pm. A song stole into the air, slowing the pace with its relaxed melody. Saffron moved to an empty table near a hedge and sat down. The red wine had numbed her senses but, although she was tired, her attention on Fenton was as taut as piano wire.

She watched the writhing dancers smooching and flirting with their partners. She suddenly thought he was coming over to her through the crowd, but no. Someone was behind him. He was leading Cassandra to the dance floor.

Saffron looked away as though the sight were too hard to watch. A cluster of firecrackers ignited and popped furiously into the night, almost jolting her out of her trance-like despair. Her intoxication was doing her no favours; her grip on her wine glass loosened and it fell to one side, spilling a trickle of red wine down her arm. She brushed it off, the spillage glistening in the frenzied lights. The night was almost over and she had not been with him because of *her*. *The bitch had it coming.*

Last orders had been called. Dancers staggered about, picking up their shoes and belongings, waving farewell. Saffron was in another world and saw none of it. A vortex of misery engulfed her as she tried to fend off a hazy dizziness inside her head. All she could do was watch Fenton from a distance as he laughed and flirted with Cassandra. He looked so happy.

A few minutes later, he came over to say goodnight to her. 'Goodnight, Saffron. I'm off now. I have work tomorrow.' He smiled at her sheepishly.

Saffron pretended she didn't care and said nothing, her eyes refusing to contact his. She felt washed out with alcohol and weak with despair. Keeping her head down, her gaze rested on his lower legs and feet. She listened to him stride away, his reluctant steps crunching the gravel. She did not see him wave at her as he walked away, his broad shoulders carrying him down the dusty street, his hair glinting in the soft glow of the street lamp.

Lifting her head wearily, she tried to focus on him. She watched his blurry outline grow smaller, then he was gone. At least he was going home alone!

Succumbing to the trauma of the night, her head fell forward. She rested her forehead on the table in front of her, letting her body drift into a blissful cocoon of alcoholic sedation. Then she surrendered to an irresistible blackness.

21

It was after eleven when they decided to leave. The music had dried up and the bar had closed. Cassandra drained the last drop from her wine glass and, accompanied by Sabina and Charity, strolled across the beer garden. She saw Saffron slumped in a plastic chair in the corner, her forehead resting on a table.

'Oh my God! Is that Saffron over there on her own?' she said, and ran over to her. Shaking Saffron's shoulder, she tried to wake her; getting no response, she tried to lift her head up whilst slapping gently at her cheek.

'Go away … leave me alone… Leave me,' growled Saffron, trying to push Cassandra's arm away.

Then Sabina and Charity were on the scene and managed to get her to her feet. All around them, party revellers danced past them into the moonlit street, not wanting the night to end. Their laughing and banter echoed down the road until their voices faded into the distance.

'Come on, Saffron,' said Sabina. 'I think you've had a bit too much tonight, love.'

Even though Cassandra knew she was being snubbed, she was still concerned for Saffron's welfare. 'She can't find her way home in that state. Look at her – she's absolutely wasted.'

'We'll take her to the caravan,' said Sabina. 'She can stay there until morning. Are you both up for that?'

Charity pulled her face. 'Do we have to?'

Cassandra, surrendering to the futility of finding an alternative option, agreed.

As they struggled down the high street, a black sky held the amber moon in place, illuminating the pathway to the meadow and beyond. They paid no heed to the reedy tune being played around them by insects still partying in the long-grassed meadow. Nor were they aware that they were being followed.

Cassandra climbed into the caravan. She was elated by too many Chardonnays and a deep satisfaction at how the evening had played out. Until Saffron, that is. Placing three mugs on the worktop, she switched on the kettle.

Charity and Sabina were struggling to navigate Saffron up the wooden steps and into the caravan. Positioning her over the bed, they released their grip and let her collapse face down onto it.

The lamps gave a soft cosy glow to the interior. Kicking off their shoes, Sabina and Charity sat down and relished the peace and quiet only a lonely gypsy caravan in a moonlit meadow could bring.

Cassandra finished making the coffee then sat down.

'What an end to a fantastic night,' said Sabina. 'Although I'm a bit concerned about Saffron.'

'I didn't realise she was drinking that much.' Cassandra blew on her coffee.

'I know enough about Saffron to know it's not like her to get into such a state. I've never seen her like this before.' Sabina sighed heavily. 'All we can do is offer her our care and hospitality and let her sleep it off.'

'Where will we sleep?' said Charity, quite miffed and pulling a face.

'I'm sure you can squeeze in on either side of her. That bed is big enough, you know!' Sabina said. They would have to make do.

'Well, I don't want to be around when she wakes up,' said Charity. 'She's been giving me evils all night.'

'I think something is bothering her.' Pausing, Sabina turned around to look at Saffron sprawled unconscious on the bed, half-hidden in the shadows. 'I have a bad feeling about this.'

Charity gave her mother a strange look. 'Another one?'

Sabina laughed. 'I don't think she's been in her right mind all evening. I can sense it.'

'Mum, why do you think she's out of her mind? She's just drunk, that's all.'

'No, it is not that,' said Sabina. 'Somethings not right.' She looked at Cassandra with her concerned, changeable green eyes. 'I am worried what might ensue.'

***

Concealing himself behind a cluster of bushy trees, Ruben Capricornus looked at the yellow glow of the caravan shining like a lantern. The blinds had not been closed and he could make out their forms moving around within. It was quiet now; the hum of insect life swarming in the long grasses vibrated a gentle tune into the night, smothering any voices.

He stood there, watching them in the caravan for at least ten minutes. Then, growing tired, he made his way back knowing Saffron would not be returning home tonight.

22

Sedated and exhausted by the sticky heat and her overindulgence of red wine, Saffron slowly began to wake up. She was horrified to find out where she was. Being sandwiched between Charity and Cassandra made her feel violated and sick, and she was keen to get away.

It was not quite dawn, and a milky grey twilight loomed outside the windows. Afraid to wake them both, she managed to stand. Holding her throbbing head, she cupped her mouth over the sink tap and gulped away her overwhelming thirst. Then, with the stealth of a black panther, she slipped outside into the meadow and fled into the early morning.

Once home at the farm house, she tackled the stairs then staggered across to the bathroom. Underpants, socks and wet towels littered the floor, and she stood on them as she sat on the toilet. Annoyingly, the roll of toilet paper was spent, a cardboard tube in its place. *Lazy bastards,* she thought, hating the fact she had to share living space with her untidy brothers.

She heard heavy footsteps on the landing. 'I'm in the bathroom,' she yelled, quickly alerting whoever was there.

It was Sam. 'Come on! Be quick in there, I'm dying out here.'

After taking her time, she opened the door to confront him. 'It's a bloody mess in here,' she said. 'Have you left it like that?' As she walked to her bedroom, she didn't see him pulling faces behind her back.

Watching her stomp away, he yelled, 'You're in a good mood. What's up with you?'

She slammed the door hard shut. It was 5.10am. After sleeping until eleven, she awoke, not refreshed but eager to put her sinister plans into action without further delay.

23

A few leisurely days had passed when Cassandra awoke in the caravan, greeted not by the sun but by an amber moon peering in through the window, illuminating her face with a golden hue. Stars were twinkling beside it, keeping it company.

Charity was nowhere to be seen. Realising she was alone, Cassandra ran to the porch wondering where she'd gone. Lights shone through the tiny cottage windows of the end cottage in the distance.

It felt eerily quiet, but she'd had a lazy day in the caravan and, after drinking a glass of wine, the warmth of the evening had numbed her into an early slumber. Her throat was dry; she needed a caffeine fix. She switched on the kettle and glanced out of the open window. A soft, fragrant breeze whispered in from the meadow.

A lamp illuminated the caravan's fairy-tale interior. She sighed, feeling relaxed and blessed. Her soul was dancing, melting with the earthy scents sneaking in from the fields – then she suddenly had an overwhelming feeling that something strange was about to happen.

She heard a rustling in the grass outside and tiptoed onto the front porch. Silhouetted against the light of the moon, a stag moved gently through the meadow, wearing its huge antlers with pride like a flamboyant, glorious crown. He was so close to her she could almost smell his breath. He was innocently sharing the comforting solitude of her own private world ... or was she in his world? *How wonderful*, she thought.

Then, as the kettle came to the boil inside the caravan, he was spooked and she watched him disappear, his outline just a shadow as he made his escape into the cover of Dead Man's Wood.

Making herself a coffee, she sat on one of the cushioned seats on the porch. Suddenly, she thought she heard someone – or something – approaching from the other side of the meadow along the snaking path from the high street.

She stood up so quickly she almost spilled her coffee. She waited on the porch, thinking it might be the stag wandering back but knew in an instant that she was wrong.

Saffron was approaching the caravan, her long hair twisted and glossy in the moonlight, her multi-coloured dress hugging her shapely figure and her silver bracelets and jewellery teasing starlight flickers around her. She was holding something in her hands.

'Hi, Cassandra,' she said. 'I hope it's not too late, but I wanted to thank you for letting me stay the other night. It's a little peace offering.' She handed Cassandra a chunky bottle plugged by a cork. 'It's sloe gin. I made it last autumn, but it matures with age. It's very sweet, just like you.'

Cassandra thought Saffron's smile forceful and fake. She felt an uncomfortable energy pulsate the air but could do nothing but accept the gift.

Saffron stood motionless waiting for a reply; she was biting her bottom lip, her lipstick a garish red. Cassandra noticed her eyes greedily feeding on the interior of the caravan, devouring the space inside.

Cassandra decided to ignore her sarcastic tone. 'You didn't have to, but that's really nice of you.' She really wanted to tell her to get lost.

Saffron glared at her with friendliness too phoney for Cassandra to take seriously. 'It's what friends are for. No trouble.'

'I've just made a coffee. Would you like one?' Cassandra was angry with herself for being so polite.

'No, I have to go to work. It was just a quick visit to say thanks, that's all.' Then she turned and wandered away down the winding path to re-join the high street.

Cassandra felt cold prickles down her back, as though the weather had suddenly changed from warm sun to frost. She had sensed Saffron's mood and decided something didn't sit well. Curiously, she looked at the bottle. A white label had been glued on it with the words in handwritten scroll: *SLOE GIN.*

A while later, Charity returned from the cottage and apologised for leaving her for so long. 'Sorry, sorry, Mum wanted me for something.'

'Oh, it's okay. I've just had a visitor and she brought me a present.'

'Who was that then?' Charity scrutinised the bottle of deep-purple liquid.

'Saffron.'

'Really? You're kidding me!'

'No, I'm not. She wanted to say thanks for the other night when we put her up.'

'And she gave you this?' Charity held up the bottle to the light. 'Sloe gin? Mum makes it sometimes before Christmas and we give it as presents. I think it's a bit sickly, but you might like it.' Then she started laughing. 'Hey, be careful. She might have poisoned it!'

They both fell silent and looked at one another. Charity's joke revealed Cassandra's own fears that she had wanted to ignore.

Sabina's welcome voice sliced through the tension as she climbed the creaky wooden steps. 'Hi there. How are you doing, Cassandra?' She'd brought some biscuits and extra tea-bags. 'It's your last week here before you move into your lovely re-vamped cottage.'

'Yes, the carpets go in this week. I hope my bed has survived – I got the builder to cover it with tarpaulin whilst everything was being done.'

'Will you miss the caravan?' Sabina asked.

'Yes, of course, but I'm looking forward to moving in. We'll still be in touch,' promised Cassandra.

Sabina picked up the bottle. 'What's this? Sloe gin? Where did you get it?'

Charity answered before Cassandra. 'It's a peace offering from Saffron for the other night. She said it was her way of saying thank you for helping her last Saturday when she was pissed.'

Cassandra laughed. 'Those were not her exact words.'

Sabina held the bottle tightly and instructed, 'Do not drink it.'

24

That night, deep sleep took Cassandra into a sinister dream that was so real it didn't feel like a dream at all. The stag was rustling in the grass outside the caravan window, and she tiptoed to the porch and watched it by the light of the moon. She went into the meadow; an ocean of flowers, alive with insect life playing a rhythmic tune.

She followed the stag through the waving foliage towards Dead Man's Wood. Its smooth fur was burgundy in the glow of the lunar light, and its mighty antlers were silhouetted. She followed him slowly into the dense trees where the top branches bent over like a woven roof. The hoot of a barn owl and a scurrying in the undergrowth were her only companions, together with a delicate breeze that gifted the night with earthy scents.

Suddenly spooked, the stag bolted into the maze of trees leaving Cassandra alone in suffocating darkness. A fire shone brightly ahead of her; moving closer, she saw a woman in long dress holding a flaming torch. Then she heard the growls and snarls of hungry wolves all around, desperate for food. She was slowly surrounded by the pack, and they were ready for the kill.

She looked at the woman, whose face was illuminated by the torch's fiery glow. Those eyes and that hair cascading down like tumbling rope, were unmistakable.

It was Saffron.

Cassandra moved closer and saw the flames reflected in Saffron's eyes, yellow and red spears dancing in two pools of liquid chocolate. She was smiling, but there was someone behind her concealed by the trunk of a fat oak tree.

Squawks and howls pierced the tension. The flaming torch revealed the impish face of a man with pale blue eyes and a wispy, white goatee beard. His thin lips were smiling, his skin flawless, but he didn't have the eyes of a human. His black pupils were thick horizontal slits like those of a goat. The face of the devil?

Then Cassandra was running, fuelled by fear, but she knew she could not outrun the wolf pack that was hot on her scent. Their synchronised killing instincts were too sophisticated and fast for her to survive – she would be ripped apart.

She felt the weight of their bodies on top of her as they pulled her down. Crushed and winded, she inhaled wet, warm blood and the stench of the wolves' breath and spittle.

Suddenly, a strong male voice commanded, 'Brandy, Milo, here now!'

She awoke suddenly to find two cocker spaniels on top of her, licking her face and rolling on the bed as if eager to please. 'Oh, my God,' she said, sitting up and trying to brush them away. Was she still dreaming?

Then there was that voice again, 'Brandy, Milo, here. Now!' It sounded like Fenton. Realising her vulnerability, she quickly pulled on her nightgown and tidied her short hair, not wanting to be seen in such a groggy state – especially by him.

Pushing open the door, she almost bumped into him. Fenton had scaled the steps and his face so close to hers that she could smell his minty toothpaste breath. He was shocked. 'Oh, Cassandra, I'm so sorry. I didn't know you were staying here.'

He looked behind her and his two cheeky spaniels brushed past her legs and ran back outside to frolic in the meadow.

Charity mumbled from the bed, 'Who's that? What's up?'

Cassandra shouted, 'It's alright, it's Fenton with his two mad dogs.'

'I am so sorry about that,' he said. 'They must have pushed open the door. I had no idea anyone was staying here or I would have kept them on the leash. Have they done any damage?'

'Nothing apart from giving me a rude awakening!'

They laughed. Charity, lifting her head and watching their conversation from the bed, was not impressed. She snuggled back into the sheets again and put her head on the pillow.

'Would you like to come in for a coffee?' asked Cassandra.

'No, I wouldn't dare. I have to get these two unruly mutts home. But thank you – we'll make another date.'

'Yes, that would be nice.'

The sun was slowly ascending, glowing gently behind a silver blanket of cloud. Fenton smiled hesitantly and said, 'How long are you here for?'

'Just until I move into my cottage this Friday.'

'So soon? If you need help with moving, I can get an hour or so off work.'

'I'm fine with everything. I'm buying new furniture so there's nothing much to move.'

Then he said those words she'd been longing to hear, 'What are you doing tonight?'

'Not much. Packing mainly.'

'Let me take you for a drink in the Green Man by way of an apology.'

He looked slightly nervous, so she didn't keep him waiting. 'That would be lovely.'

'About seven?'

'Seven, it is.' She smiled, not revealing a hint of the happiness swirling inside her.

Putting his dogs safely on a leash, Fenton said, 'I'll meet you there at seven.'

She watched him melt into the distance and eventually disappear into the high street.

25

The day was steadily heating up. Cassandra left the doors and windows wide open and lifted one of the cushioned chairs to the shady side of the caravan. Cooling herself with a glass of icy lemonade, she noticed how quickly the ice dissolved into nothing.

She watched cabbage-white butterflies dance and insects dart and swim; their colours iridescent. She couldn't wait for this evening and she wondered what to wear – something cool but not too revealing, casual yet sophisticated.

She couldn't believe how wonderful she felt. The anticipation of meeting Fenton and wondering what might ensue made her blush and smile.

Taking another gulp of her lemonade, she noticed someone approaching on the horizon. It was Saffron, her hair a shock of red reflecting the sunlight. She was walking quickly and her face held a sour despair.

'Hi Saffron. You, okay?' she asked.

Saffron folded her arms across her chest and glared at her. 'I hear you're meeting Fenton tonight at the pub.'

'Yes, that's right, just for a drink.'

'You do realise he is my boyfriend and off limits?'

'He never said – but it's only a drink to apologise for his dogs barging into the caravan this morning. I had no…'

Saffron didn't let her finish her sentence. 'You really expect me to believe you? I've seen you flirting with him, so don't play the innocent with me.' Her face was flushed with anger.

Cassandra didn't know what to say. Fenton hadn't said a thing about Saffron being his girlfriend; besides, she remembered Sabina saying he was single and Saffron was only a friend. 'It is only a drink. I thought you were just friends.'

'Well, you thought wrong, so stay off if you know what's good for you.'

'Please, Saffron, just sit down. I'll get another chair.'

'I don't want to sit down with you. Back off, alright? Or else.' She turned and marched away through the beautiful meadow that didn't look so beautiful any more.

Shocked, Cassandra went inside the caravan. Her heart was beating fast. Gulping the last of the lemonade, she locked the doors and windows and then went to Sabina's shop.

Trudging along the path, she was confused by the encounter. Maybe Saffron was a little insane and was deluded about Fenton being her boyfriend. She had noticed the unpredictability in the girl's eyes. What was an insanely jealous person capable of doing? Saffron had already given her the sloe gin – what if it really were poisoned? Cassandra didn't want to believe it. Things like that didn't happen, not in the real world.

Anxiously, she entered the shop, scarcely noticing its beautiful aromas and soothing music. Charity was behind the counter.

'Is your mum, around?' Cassandra asked.

'What's up? You look troubled – are you okay?'

'Yeah, but I need to talk to her.'

Sabina appeared from the back of the shop. She was saying goodbye to a middle-aged lady who had just had a tarot reading. Charity waved to get her attention. 'What is it? What's wrong?' Sabina asked as they went into the back room.

When Cassandra told her, she was equally shocked. 'That doesn't make any sense. They aren't together.'

'She was quite adamant. She warned me off him and threatened me with something nasty if I didn't leave him alone. Fenton asked me for a drink and I accepted because I thought he was single. He's not leading me on, is he?'

'I doubt it. Anyway, are you going to let her dictate what you do? If he's asked you out for a drink, what the hell is it to do with her? You have to make a stand and show her she doesn't have a say. If they do have a romantic relationship, why would he take you to the Green Man pub of all places? She works there! Show her who's boss – you go and don't let her intimidate you.'

Cassandra knew Sabina was right; she'd just needed some reassurance. She would meet Fenton tonight as arranged and blow the consequences. Besides, what could Saffron do?

She headed back to the caravan to seek refuge in the shade once again.

26

Later that afternoon, Cassandra stood in the mini-shower and let tepid soapy water cleanse away the sticky heat of the day. She felt cautiously optimistic about tonight; she would enjoy herself, no matter what transpired.

Dressing in a cool linen dress then dusting her face with a whisper of makeup, she painted her lips a gentle pink as she waited impatiently for the clock to say 6.45. Slipping on her sandals, and with her purse and phone in a small bag, she set off to the pub.

A fresh breeze kept her temperature down and her spirits up. She was nervous – or was it just excitement? She decided on the latter.

The interior of the Green Man seemed to greet her with a welcoming energy. She knew instinctively that so many souls had passed through this doorway over the centuries, each of them leaving behind an invisible presence.

She saw Fenton at the bar waiting for her, pint in hand. He turned and smiled; their date had begun.

He ordered her a large glass of wine and they sat by the window. It was then that she noticed his true eye colour: not just blue, but with a greeny-hazel centre that complemented his complexion. He had tried to impress her; he smelled of fresh soap with just a hint of something sensuous.

'I'm thinking of having a housewarming party on Saturday for a few friends. I'd love you to come,' Cassandra said, hypnotised by his eyes. 'It'll start about seven.'

He smiled back. 'Just try and keep me away.'

'Sabina and Charity are coming. It's only a little get together to welcome new energy into the house. Sabina is bringing sage with her to cleanse and bless the rooms with positive vibes.'

'Is Saffron going too?'

Cassandra didn't know quite what to say. Looking down at her glass of cold wine, she said, 'No, I don't think so. To be honest, I don't think she likes me that much.'

'That's crazy. How could anyone not like you?'

'When I came here to the village, I thought that you and she were an item.'

'What, me and Saff?' He laughed. 'No way. We're friends, but we are more like brother and sister. I've known her all my life. We even went to the same schools.'

Cassandra realised that he had missed all the signs. Had he mistaken romantic idealisation for mere sisterliness? She felt an uneasy tingle travel up her spine. Saffron must be totally deluded – and maybe even dangerous.

***

Seething, Saffron watched them. They were laughing and talking, and she felt her insides sear with anger and frustration. She was hiding in the kitchen, peering through the glass door into the bar area.

Although not working that evening, she had made an excuse to come back. Frank was behind the bar serving a cluster of customers. She left by the back kitchen door to return home, a wave of anger pushing her all the way. Things were not working out as she had imagined. She needed to see the hag again.

***

Cassandra and Fenton left the pub around 9.30pm. He wanted to see her back to the caravan and she accepted, hoping he would stay a while. Dusky haze painted the sky, hiding the moon as they walked across the meadow. Suddenly he took hold of her hand, the warm texture of his polished palm against hers, then he gently pulled her to him and kissed her full on the lips. They embraced instinctively.

He looked into her eyes. 'I've been dying to do that all night. You are so beautiful.'

She began to melt inside with a vulnerability she didn't really welcome. She was not in control, but she was in rapture.

They continued along the path to the caravan. Cassandra hoped Charity had remembered not to be there so she and Fenton could be alone. Once inside, she tried to regain her normal composure and made coffee.

Fenton suddenly pulled her to him and they continued where they left off. At around midnight he left, but not before giving her one more kiss on her neck, on her naked breasts and on her full, hungry lips.

'Until Saturday,' he said. 'I'm counting down the hours already.' Like a forbidden lover, he stole back through the meadow, leaving Cassandra with a sensuous afterglow she had never encountered before.

27

The next morning, fuelled by jealous rage and desperation, Saffron flung herself into the dense maze of Dead Man's Wood. She had to see the hag.

Making her way along the path next to the almost-dry stream, she projected her thoughts into the ether to summon the hag, her gift of wine heavy in the bag that bounced against her thigh. The sun was not yet radiating its welcome heat, and she shivered as goose bumps twitched at her skin.

'Are you there?' she whispered. Her only companions were the soldier-like trees standing to attention, their branches and leaves waving like arms in the breeze.

The temperature shifted down a notch and the atmosphere plunged into a different dimension. The hag was there, looking at her, almost concealed by one of the lofty trees. She moved closer to Saffron whilst firmly sucking on her clay pipe. As she spoke, splinters of corroded teeth moved in unison with her words. 'You again. What is it now?' She squinted curiously.

Saffron slowly moved forward, placed the bottle of red wine on the ground then stepped back, hoping to get her approval. Whilst she was wondering how to word her enquiry, the hag spoke.

'It isn't working, is it?' she said. 'And ye think it can when the fates wish otherwise? Ye cannot force destiny. What makes ye so special, girl, as to want to change the fates?' She continued to chew on her clay pipe as she waited for a response. 'Cat got your tongue?'

Saffron glared uncomfortably at the hag, not wanting their meeting to be a waste of time. 'But she's not right for him,' she pleaded. 'I just know it.'

'She is a seer, just like you. She has a path to walk and her initiation has begun. She has ghosts of the past to deal with, and ghosts of the dead, so she may leave if she finds things too much. Have ye tried the black salt?'

'No, not yet.'

'I do not play with the devil, lass, so I can tell ye no more. Ye can do what ye want but ye are on your own if ye push the matter further.' The old woman bent to claim her gift.

'What do you mean by ghosts of the past and the dead?' asked Saffron.

'She has a bad spirit in her new home who wishes her away, just like ye do. She has a living spirit of the past who has done her wrong. They may banish her before ye can.' The hag cackled. 'That is my answer, lass, not my advice.' With a swirling shift of energy, she was gone, back to her own time somewhere in the many dimensions of the ether.

Saffron sped home. Her only thoughts were black salt, an evil ghost in Cassandra's new home, maybe unfinished business from the past, and a creeping realisation that Cassandra had it coming. She would try the black salt next to banish her away.

Climbing the stairs, she went to her bedroom to mix the concoction of black salt for her banishing spell. She took a pestle and mortar and sprinkled rock salt into it, crushing it into a fine powder. She retrieved some ashes from her sage cleansing bowl and added the mixture, blending the contents to form a gritty, dark-grey salt. She put the contents into a plastic bag; before placing it in her tote bag, she held it between her palms and sent an intention to banish Cassandra once and for all.

In the kitchen downstairs it was a flurry of activity as Sam and Joe competed for space whilst making their breakfast. Saffron ignored their irritable banter. As she sipped her coffee, she relished her next move. Leaving her empty mug on the kitchen table, she sped into the bright morning.

28

The morning brought a welcome coolness, a hazy sky and a wispy breeze, respite from the clutches of the prolonged heat of this early summer. Yesterday had been nothing but a daze for Cassandra. The afterglow of the previous night still shimmered inside her.

She would give Saffron a wide berth from now on. She'd always had a sense of something not quite right with the girl, but she had crossed a line. Cassandra felt sad that wherever she went in the world evil lurked somewhere.

Pushing open the caravan door, she allowed the fresh sweet breeze entry. All her belongings were packed and ready to go, and she felt welcome butterflies in her tummy at the thought of moving into the cottage. She couldn't wait to get the keys. Mark the builder was meeting her there at 9am so she could inspect the work and pay him.

It was 8.46am as she set off into the fledgling morning. On the high street, life was slowly gaining momentum into another perfect day. The delicious scent from the tea shop held the smell of cooked English breakfasts and ground coffee.

Looking ahead, she approached her cottage. As she grew nearer, she felt a rush of excitement. Although the front garden was flat and parched, the skip had gone. The stone elevation looked pristine with its new pointing and had been sandblasted, the old skin of stone exfoliated to reveal pale, virgin stone.

Along the path, she noticed an offshoot of a rambling rose trying to anchor itself to the wall, reclaiming its destiny to adorn the frontage with blushes of splendour later in the year.

Mark was waiting at the door with a smile on his face. 'Hi, Cassandra,' he said, as he jangled the keys teasingly in front of her nose. 'Are you ready for this? Here you go.'

When she crossed the threshold, odours of fresh paint and raw wood tickled her nose. The stone floor was still intact, pointed with new grouting. The rickety staircase looked fresh from the many timber operations it had endured, but it enhanced the atmosphere with its presence. The steps and risers had been dressed with a soft oatmeal carpet. The doors had been sanded down and painted eggshell-white, and every wall shone with a whitewashed hue.

Walking into the living room, Cassandra noticed the old Christmas card propped up on the new mantle. 'Ah, the Christmas card you found,' she said. 'I'd forgotten about that.' Replacing it, she walked into the kitchen and gasped at its beauty. The glare from the shiny black worktop almost took her breath away.

Mark opened the top half of the kitchen stable door and a breeze kissed the interior. As Cassandra went upstairs, she noticed the staircase did not protest as before; its temperament had been hypnotised from cantankerous irritability into a deep slumber. The carpet continued onto the landing and into the bedrooms, where light shone through the new windows making each room appear bigger and brighter.

The bathroom door opened into a spa-like interior. Not unlike a five-star hotel suite, the room dazzled with bright clean tiles and bathroom furniture. Slate-grey tiles adorned the floor and a huge mirror on the side wall made it look double the size. Everywhere was gleaming with light.

Feeling ecstatic, Cassandra followed Mark back down the stairs. 'I will transfer your money,' she said, 'I am so happy with everything, and you've worked so hard.'

'Any problems, just give me a call no matter what time. Sometimes there are snags we can't anticipate, so you know where you can find me. Good luck with everything, love.'

'Thanks, Mark.'

The front door closed gently behind him and she found herself alone. The stable door was still open as she sat at her kitchen table and slowly scanned the perfection that was now her new home.

Then she thought she saw something move past the back window, but she could have been mistaken. Peering out from the open stable door into the garden, she saw nothing but a forest of shambolic weeds competing for dominance with the struggling shrubs and grasses.

She returned inside to her peaceful solitude, only to be interrupted by a tapping noise coming from the hidden recess of her utility space. As she edged closer, it continued. It sounded like someone hammering on a lead pipe down a mine shaft. But how could that be?

As she pulled at the silver handle of the door to open it, an icy blast blistered up her arm. The recess revealed itself to her and a smudgy blackness beckoned. She flicked the light switch and the space flooded with bright light, showing nothing but the shiny washer-dryer and shelves above. The noise had stopped, but she was thinking of the ghoulish squatter residing somewhere in the house. Surely Mark would have noticed something and told her? There was nothing there.

The sun crept into the back garden, lifting her suspicious mood. She watched a young girl on horseback ride slowly along the rear bridleway, the horse's earthy, leathery smell tainting the air with its comforting presence. The girl turned to smile at her, and the horse snorted in greeting as they moved on.

Her troubled mind diluted by the encounter, Cassandra sat on a stone step among the weeds. The slow, rhythmic noise of the horse's hooves grew faint as it trudged steadily away into the distance, giving her a sense of comforting reassurance that all was well.

29

Just after five, Sabina and Charity knocked at Cassandra's new oak door.

'Come in,' Cassandra shouted. 'The door is open.'

Walking down the hallway, they looked in awe at the interior of the cottage. 'This is beautiful,' said Sabina. 'They've done an excellent job. I never expected anything so wonderful. Who would have thought it?' She was wide-eyed with admiration.

Charity walked through the hallway into the kitchen, but Sabina paused and stopped to look at the bizarre staircase with its inconsistent treads and risers. As she held on to the banister, her stare followed its twisting spine to the top of the landing. Suddenly a surge of sickening fear pierce her gut, and she immediately let go.

Not wanting to upset Cassandra, she left her experience unspoken and entered the sunny, whitewashed kitchen. 'It's lovely, and so bright,' she said, trying to brush away her unease.

'Tea? Coffee?' Cassandra clattered some cups onto the worktop and switched on the kettle.

'I'd love a coffee.' Charity placed a box of biscuits on the table. 'These are for you.' She started quizzing Cassandra about the previous night. 'Are you going to tell us about your date with Fenton?' she asked. 'What happened? Did it go well?'

Cassandra smiled coyly. 'Yes, it went very well.' She tried not to blush. 'In fact, it was amazing – *he's* amazing. He's coming to the housewarming on Saturday, and I can't wait to see him again.'

'I knew it,' said Sabina, her fingers teasing the crystal hanging from its chain on her chest. 'A match made in heaven.'

'I just hope it's the real thing and I'm not getting carried away again.'

'Life is to be lived fully, Cassandra. If it is meant to be, it will be. Go with the flow and stop doubting yourself. You have to take risks, that is what life is all about otherwise what is the point of it? Like the old saying goes, a ship is safe in the harbour but that is not what it was meant for.'

Charity stood up to finish her coffee, leaving Cassandra at the table with her mother.

'Do you think Saffron really poisoned that bottle of sloe gin and she means me harm?' asked Cassandra, wincing at the possibility.

'Well, I wouldn't rule it out. If she did, let's see what she does when a few weeks pass and you're still fine.'

'Come on, I'll show you the rest of the house.'

Cassandra led the way into the living room. Sabina instinctively homed in on the Christmas card on the mantle. 'It's a bit early for Christmas cards, isn't it?' She held the stained item to the light cascading through the window and delicately pulled it open to reveal the message inside. 'Flo, Agnes and Lilly. Were these the previous owners, I wonder?'

'I don't know. The builder found it on the staircase during the renovations. It must have sneaked out from a hidden crack. I think it's quite cute.'

Sabina had fallen into a void of heightened sensitivity, and her eyes glazed to a pale green as she held the card. Cassandra and Charity were looking through the front window onto the high street when she spoke. 'I don't think they've all moved out,' she said, her stare trance-like.

They both spun around to face her. 'What was that?' said Cassandra.

'They are still here,' Sabina replied, holding on to her crystal. 'I feel a presence in the house, at least one other spirit, maybe two. Can I go upstairs?'

'Please do,' replied Cassandra, uneasy that her new home might still have supernatural squatters.

The staircase didn't make a sound as Sabina ascended. She walked forward cautiously, letting her sixth sense guide her. A heavy force of sadness lured her into the front bedroom.

The newly refurbished space concealed something chilling, an undulating force from another time dimension under its new façade. It slowly revealed itself, and a hazy grey mass stretched into the corner of the room. A hooded, hunched figure of a woman was staring at her with pinprick pupils, pulling on her life-force energy as though feeding from her.

'Who are you, and what do you want?' demanded Sabina.

116

It replied with a hissing rush of spite, its energy vulgar and cruel. 'Get out, get out!' it said. 'This is my house! I am the eldest! I am the next of kin! This house belongs to me.'

Sabina replied sternly, but with caution. 'Don't you know you are dead and have no right in the world? You must move into the light. Why didn't you move into the light?'

'What light do you talk of? Get out, get out now,' it said, its voice echoey and strained.

'I shall not. It is you who must go.' Like the strong roots of an oak tree, Sabina asserted her right to be in the earthly realm and grounded herself in the room, imagining her feet anchoring her deep into the earth.

'Me? Me? Never,' the spectre said, then came a piercing squeal of frustration from its twisted mass. It moved like a huge black rat, scurrying across the carpet along the skirting-board and disappeared through the wall. There was silence, and the suffocating energy was replaced by a normal glow once more. But Sabina knew she had not seen the last of this evil entity.

Charity and Cassandra were waiting patiently at the bottom of the stairs, knowing Sabina had encountered something. Sabina looked over the banister and shouted, 'It's alright, it's gone for now.'

Congregating on the landing, they looked around them but could see nothing but bright daylight illuminating the freshly painted rooms. 'What was it? Who was it?' asked Cassandra.

'It's a stubborn one, but I've come across this kind before. We may need a ritual to move it into the light, but we have to be firm with it. This is your house, Cassandra, but I fear the spirit may be a bully and think that you are soft. You must assert yourself and put it in its place.' Running her hands along the banister, she continued, 'If it turns up again, don't be intimidated. Show them who's boss. I will get my cleansing sage.'

Unravelling a dry bundle of the herb from a cotton cloth in her bag, she lit the end of it. As she blew gently on the flames, it settled into a red-tipped glow producing swirls of pungent smoke. Holding it over an abalone shell to catch the falling cinders, Sabina stroked the smoke around the rooms with a large white feather.

Cassandra and Charity looked on as the spirals of smoke invaded each room and Sabina mumbled an indecipherable incantation under her breath. Her breathing was deep and heavy, and there was a faraway glaze in her green eyes.

She cleansed the landing and all the way down the twisted staircase. When she went into the living room, she took hold of the Christmas card and let swirls of grey smoke envelop it to wash away any negativity. Once in the kitchen, she was immediately pulled towards the utility cupboard. Opening its doors, she plunged the smouldering sage into its void. A noise not of this world wailed a protest from inside; echoey and high pitched, it sounded far away in another dimension. Sabina hoped it would get the message.

She placed the smoking sage stick into the abalone shell and tapped it gently to extinguish its embers. 'That is all I can do for now, but I feel it may have moved on. Let's hope and pray that it has.'

'What if it appears to me again and shouts in my ear? I don't think I can cope with that,' said Cassandra.

'Nonsense! Stick up for yourself, Cassandra. You are more powerful than you realise. You are meant to be here, ghosts are not. The spectre is the weak one, the intruder in this world. It has nothing to anchor itself except a spiteful sense of entitlement to what is now yours. You must tell it in no uncertain terms to leave.'

Cassandra smiled but felt no joy. 'I'll try,' she said.

After finishing their lukewarm coffee, Sabina and Charity left. As the front door softly closed, Cassandra found herself alone once again, the excitement and elation of unpacking in her new home had somehow left her.

***

As evening came, Cassandra kept herself busy. She had been looking forward to moving in, yet now the sweet anticipation had turned sour. As the night crawled in, dimming the daylight from the windows, she switched on the lights and turned on the radio on the window sill. Suddenly she felt a pang of homesickness for the caravan. *How stupid of me.*

She went upstairs and dressed her bed with fresh sheets, ready to move in permanently tomorrow. As she walked downstairs, she noticed the tune on the radio had changed to a 1967 hit called 'Somebody to Love'. She thought of Fenton, his rugged skin and cheeky grin, and their night of passion in the caravan. Her mood lifted to one of anticipation at seeing him at her house warming.

Switching off all the lights, she locked up and ran along the high street, across the meadow to the caravan, its bed a welcome respite from the spooky goings-on in her cottage. She decided she would move in tomorrow, squatting spectre or no squatting spectre.

30

The morning blessed the meadow with its sweet warmth, subtly caressing the abundant wildlife. Tiny flies, bees and butterflies swam through the sea of colour, basking in the long shoots and grasses as though celebrating their magical existence.

Cassandra sipped her tea and sat on the porch, knowing this would be her last morning in this fairy-tale abode. As she packed her sparse belongings, she bent down to pick up her sandals. One of them had been violated with a gritty splash of dirt. She held it upside down; a powdery, dry mixture poured down like a sandy waterfall and was taken by the subtle breeze and washed away into the meadow.

She knew about this witchery: black salt in the shoes. Was it a banishment spell? She automatically thought of Saffron. Had Saffron been here with evil intent, prowling around to exercise her manipulative spells?

An uncomfortable chill ran through her, but she brushed it off. She was leaving the caravan today and the spell had been futile – she was moving on anyway.

Was it Saffron who had nailed the dolls onto Sabina's back gate? Noticing the bottle of sloe gin unopened on the table, Cassandra stuffed it into one of her bags. Although she knew she'd never drink it, it might be dangerous and she wanted it out of the way of any unsuspecting victims.

After cleaning the bathroom, kitchen and floors, she locked up and went back to her cottage. She paused halfway to look at the beauty of the caravan, then her mind filled with the memory of Fenton and the passion they had shared there. She would miss her gypsy retreat.

Approaching her cottage from the high street, she was disappointed to see her weird old friend, Bill the tramp, standing outside. As she opened the garden gate, he approached her. 'You can't go in there,' he said. 'Them witches will get you. Don't you know there's witches in there?' He was struggling to be coherent.

Oh my God, here we go again. Cassandra glared at him with annoyance and rested her bag on the garden wall. 'I live here now, this is my new home. Do you like it?'

'No, them, witches live there. You can't go in, they'll not be happy.'

'There are no witches, only me.' She smiled and continued up the path. Thrusting her key in the door, she opened it.

'Agnes will not be happy. She'll chase you away with her broom. She did that when we were kids … you can't go in there.' He swayed and glared at her with that toothless grin that had scared her so much the first time she'd seen him.

Cassandra, trying to humour him, replied, 'Yes, alright, thank you.' Pausing at the threshold, she watched him shuffle away along the street, talking to himself.

Inside, she went into the living room where the Christmas card was still upright on the mantle. She read it again:

Happy Christmas
Flo, Agnes and Lilly
With love Mary xxx

Who had lived here before – were they all witches? She laughed, but her eye was drawn to the name on the card. Bill had said the name Agnes; maybe he'd known the last occupants many years ago? However, he was a bit of a nutter.

Turning on the radio in the kitchen, she filled the house with soft music interspersed with banter from the DJ. She was getting things ready for the housewarming party tomorrow – she wanted to make a good impression, especially as Fenton would be there. She tried to push away intrusive thoughts, but failed.

The stable door was open and she watched as two ponies went by along the bridle path, trudging steadily up the track accompanied by the dance of a few red admiral butterflies. Their riders were relaxed in their saddles, allowing the slow pace to take them comfortably up to the fields beyond.

Cassandra had ordered some groceries from the supermarket in the next town, and they covered her kitchen worktops with bags of unpacked food, home essentials and several bottles of wine. She was eager to use her new wine chiller and proudly stacked them inside, amused at the elation it provoked. She stored away the food into the fridge and cupboards. Cold sausage rolls and sandwiches would be on the menu, with wine or beer.

Once she had done all she could, she sat at the kitchen table with a cup of tea and cheese sandwich. Nothing but the noise of nature intruded from outside, the hum of bumble bees subtly interspersed with birdsong. Morning slipped into afternoon then into evening; opening a bottle of Chardonnay, she poured a large glass and treated herself to a solitary celebration of moving into her new home.

31

Everything was ready for the party tomorrow. New towels were hanging in the bathroom and her two settees had arrived and been placed in the living room next to the wood burner in the stone fireplace, transforming it from an empty space into a relaxing retreat. There were scatter cushions along the seats, and a matching blind framed the view of the high street.

Cassandra gulped at her wine and felt a rush of elation at her achievements since the split with her fiancé, Paul. Then suddenly a rush of unwanted memories ambushed her; thoughts of where he might be in the world after defrauding her.

After forging her signature to re-mortgage her home for more than £200,000, he had fled the country with his new bitch and left her to deal with the consequences. She had only found out about the fraud a few weeks later when the mortgage company sent her an arrears letter. Her house had to be sold to pay off the debt because Paul could not be found and she could not prove she hadn't signed the agreement. Presumably he had left the country.

Her face flushed with humiliation at being so trusting. Why hadn't he told her the wedding was off? He had let her go through the charade of being jilted at the altar. Luckily, she'd had some savings and her mother had left her a trust fund which matured when she was twenty-one; that was just enough to buy and renovate the cottage.

Now she could turn her attention to the future and embrace a fresh start in Whalley Dell. She poured another glass of wine. Other people went through a lot worse in life. At least she was still there to carry on – but that didn't seem to help her feelings.

Night was closing in and she decided to have a bath. Stepping into the bubbles, the smell relaxed her and she let the fragrant liquid soak away the painful memories. She couldn't help but give a silent prayer of thanks for her chance of a fresh start in life.

Donning her robe, she crossed the landing into her bedroom. The sun had already set, leaving the bedroom dull with shadows.

The moon still shone brightly in the sky, but its effect wasn't as raw and intrusive as in the caravan.

She remembered the mysterious stag in the meadow fleetingly sharing its existence with her, and suddenly felt a tinge of sorrow. Crossing the room, she let her robe drop to the floor and threw herself onto her bed. She stretched out, welcoming the coolness of the crisp sheets. The day had been challenging, but she was relaxed now and surrendering into a deep slumber. She was looking forward to seeing Fenton tomorrow. She fell into a deep cleansing sleep.

***

When she awoke the next morning, the sun had not yet moved around to her bedroom window but she could see it shining into the street. She had slept all night on top of her bed and now felt goosebumps on her skin.

Reaching for her robe, she went to the bathroom to ready herself for the day. Once downstairs, she made coffee. The sun had not quite reached the kitchen window so she switched on the lights under the kitchen units.

In the distance, black-and-white sheep were grazing in the field beyond the bridle path. Hugging her coffee in her hands, she tried to ward off the slight chill in the air.

As she turned around, she couldn't believe what she was seeing: all her cupboard doors were suddenly wide open and the atmosphere had frozen. There was no movement or sound. She looked around her in disbelief, noticing she was holding her breath, unable to accept the scene before her. She watched as cloudy black words filled the rear wall in front of her: *GET OUT*.

Her coffee cup crashed onto the floor, spilling its contents and shattering. The splintering noise seemed to jolt the ether and suddenly a lightness came, lifting the room back to normality. The cupboard doors were no longer open, the writing was gone and she could breathe again.

Now she knew for sure that the spectre had not left. If she were to get any peace, she would have to toughen up. She decided to ask for Sabina's help; she was determined to get her home back once and for all. After her other home had been stolen from her, she would not let a ghost steal this one.

Locking up, she set off to Magic Things to relay her predicament to Sabina. It had just gone 9am and the shop was waking up, gently stretching its sleepy bones to welcome in the morning. A fledgling breeze trespassed the threshold together with Cassandra, and she heard a kettle coming to the boil in the back room and gentle voices conversing.

Sabina looked surprised. 'I wasn't expecting to see you so early. What's up?'

'It's back. It's not gone,' said Cassandra.

32

Sabina left Charity in the shop and accompanied Cassandra back to her cottage. Cassandra told her about the conversation with the tramp the previous night and the name Agnes on the Christmas card.

Crossing the threshold, Sabina braced herself for any supernatural confrontation. 'This cottage is so beautiful,' she said, 'You can't really imagine anything so horrible is here, but...' She paused. She was holding onto the handrail of the twisted staircase and she felt immense unease.

'It's upstairs again,' she said. 'Hold my hands, then we can confront this thing together. I need to home in on why it will not relinquish its claim to the house. Only then can we move it on.'

As they held hands, Sabina whispered a prayer asking that the pure white light of the Christ protect them whatever happened. Cassandra followed slowly to the top landing where all was quiet, then into the front bedroom where there was a noticeable drop in temperature. They both shivered at the unquestionable evidence that the spectre was there with them.

Sabina shouted into the room, 'Are you Agnes?'

There was no response.

Cassandra suddenly snapped and shouted loudly, 'Agnes, Agnes is that you? Why are you here? This is my home now.'

Suddenly the room seemed to implode and they found themselves plunged into a time warp. Images ran simultaneously through their minds; the spectre was showing them something.

The room turned frosty cold and they were transported back in time to a dishevelled hovel, the rundown heap the cottage had once been. Dark furniture graced raw floorboards; there was a metal-framed bed against the wall with an elderly person sleeping in it. A wet blustery draught was blowing through a gap somewhere in the rain-splattered window.

Dumfounded, Sabina and Cassandra could only surrender to the scenes playing out before them.

6 MEADOW ROW, Whalley Dell – 1958 – Flo, Agnes and Lilly

Lilly heard a loud bang from upstairs, her mother's bedroom door being slammed again, then an indecipherable sound of annoyance thundering from her older sister Agnes's mouth, loud enough to raise the dead.

It never ceased to amaze Lilly how relentlessly cruel Agnes could be to their mother, who had been sick and bedridden for six months. Her illness was elusive, with too many confusing symptoms, and the doctor had diagnosed old age. But Lilly knew it wasn't just that; it was caused by the foul treatment Mother had endured for many years at the hands of her spiteful older daughter, Agnes.

Stocky and strong, Agnes used her thick-set frame to bully both Lilly and her mother, and Lilly was getting sick of it. Although skinny, almost frail, she bravely confronted her sister from the bottom of the twisted staircase. 'Please, Agnes,' she said, stuttering slightly, 'don't be like that with her, it's not her fault.'

Agnes, spat back, 'Of course it's her fault. I'm bloody running up and down stairs all day for her. Get me this, get me that, wash my gown again. I'm sick of her fouling it! She thinks I have nothing better to do.'

'I will see to her, then. Why don't you let me?'

'You? Are you mad?' Agnes said. 'You're not capable of looking after a dead cat. You are stupid, dizzy and pathetic. You can't even look after yourself.' She looked her up and down disapprovingly. 'Just look at you! Not even dressed yet, and it must be ten already.'

Lilly moved into the kitchen out of earshot, filled the kettle with water and lit the gas on the stove. Retrieving the teapot from the cupboard, she lined up three cups on the counter.

Agnes came up behind her. Her laboured breath was hot and noisy, making the back of Lilly's neck bristle. 'Don't make her one,' she said. 'She doesn't deserve it. I am run ragged with her.'

As she threw her mother's soiled nightdress into the enamel sink, a putrid stench of vomit released into the air. 'Wash that!'

Lilly sighed, realising there was no point in disobeying her older sister. She had tried to but she couldn't handle Agnes's violence again. Better to keep the peace and not argue, she thought, her fingers stroking a grazed lump on her cheekbone.

The kettle began to whistle. Lilly hoped Agnes wouldn't notice as she made Mother a cup of tea. Agnes had gone into the front room by then, so Lilly tried to sneak it upstairs, but she was ambushed by Agnes at the bottom of the staircase.

'What did I say? I said don't make her one and you defy me! How can we have any order in this house when you disobey me?' She grabbed for the cup but Lilly held firm, not wanting it to spill or, God forbid, scald Agnes. Falling from her hand, it bounced on the stone floor, smashing its contents everywhere, painting the wall and skirting-board with a wash of beige.

'What have you done that for?' spat Agnes. 'Look at the mess. Clean it up.'

Lilly hurriedly retrieved a damp cloth from the kitchen and blotted the tea stain, still enduring her sister's rant.

'You're not even doing that right,' tutted Agnes, watching Lilly on all fours picking up the broken pieces and scrubbing at the mess. 'I am going to the shop,' she continued, squeezing her huge arms into her raincoat. 'Just make sure it's done by the time I get back.'

The wind outside reflected her fury as she slammed the door behind her. Her anger seemed to linger still in the hallway, gifting Lilly with a shock of humiliation and sadness.

She ran to the kitchen with the smashed pieces of pottery and threw them in the bin. Pouring another cup, she knew she had to be quick as she didn't know how long Agnes would be. The twisted staircase groaned in protest with every single step, a deafening annoyance from its grumpy structure.

Pushing open the door, Lilly looked into a dusty, dark room not unlike a grey prison cell. Heavy, faded curtains kept out the daylight, and the air was damp and cold with a tangy stale odour of urine. Her mother's breath, visible in the cold air, was the only indicator that she was still alive.

As Lilly placed the cup on the bedside table, the old woman asked, 'Lilly, is that you?' She opened her white, gauzy eyes.

'Yes, Mum, it's me,' said Lilly. 'I am so sorry about earlier. Here is a nice cup of tea for you.' She placed it on the bedside table. 'Agnes should not treat you like this. She won't let me help you. She's a bully.'

'Thank you,' said her mother, her voice frail. Then, with her brittle hand, she pointed to the dresser at the foot of her bed. 'Please, Lilly, love,' she said, 'get me the brown envelope from the bottom drawer. It's a big envelope underneath my sheets. It's my deeds.'

'Oh, Mum,' sighed Lilly.

'Please, it's important. Give it to me.' Her mother's twig-like finger stabbed into the darkness where the dresser stood.

Lilly retrieved the document from its hiding place. She noticed the yellowing envelope had endured the passage of time, keeping the concealed contents intact. Inside were the title deeds to the cottage, 6 Meadow Row, Whalley Dell, her mother's only valuable possession.

She handed it over and struggled to hear her mother's words as blustery rain pelted aggressively at the window and the wind whistled like a banshee screaming to be let in.

'The cottage will go to you and your sister when I die,' her mother said. 'But Agnes will do everything to take it for herself. Don't let her do that.' Her breathing was laboured and wheezy. 'I don't have much time, so listen to what I say. This house will belong to you and your sister equally so you will both have somewhere to live.'

'Oh, Mum, don't be silly. You're not leaving us anytime soon.' Lilly stroked her mother's arm but, feeling only bone and sinew, she knew her mother was right. Cradling the back of her head she lifted the teacup to her mother's dry lips. Her skull was already corpse-like, with wispy grey strands of hair peeping out from her lacy nightcap.

The old woman gulped down the warm liquid to lubricate her throat, then she let out a strange, rattling sound, sighed with satisfaction and lowered her head back onto the pillow.

Lilly felt tears gather as she remembered how her mother used to be; she had aged almost twenty years in just six months. Her eyes, bleached to icy white with cataracts, seemed to stare into the room, observing the spectral dancing shadows waltzing against the walls. She seemed to be excavating an ancient intelligence within herself, and Lilly watched the grey stillness of time entertain her mother with its rhythm. Would she soon join them in their reverie and become their friend forever?

Pushing the document into its envelope, Lilly placed it back into its hiding place. Retrieving the half-empty cup, she went quickly down the twisted staircase to wash it and hide the evidence of her betrayal.

Half an hour later, Agnes was back with a basket of groceries: a small loaf of bread, a few ounces of ham, and a tiny square of cheese. She felt compelled to apologise as she looked at Lilly who was sitting at the table, ignoring her and staring at her skinny hands as they clasped together nervously.

'Listen, sorry about earlier,' Agnes muttered. She pulled her stout, muscular arms out of her now-drenched raincoat. She left the apology to linger in the room, but the words were dissolving with their insincerity. However, the apology seemed to give Agnes a smug air of having redeemed herself, and she bounced around the kitchen clearing the groceries away, vindicated of any wrongdoing. A stench of damp lingered around, dragged in from the rain outside, mingling distastefully with her musty body odour.

'Right!' she said, her tone upbeat. 'Would you like a cup of tea, Lilly?' She was enjoying her feeling of superiority.

'Yes,' said Lilly.

Agnes snapped back like a school teacher, 'Yes what?'

'Yes, please.'

Agnes banged the kettle clumsily against the sink then onto the gas stove. 'There is no excuse for bad manners, Lilly,' she said bossily. 'They don't cost anything!'

When the kettle whistled, she filled the pot and poured tea into three cups. Placing a handful of biscuits on a plate, she handed them to Lilly with the tea. 'There now, you can take this up to Mother,' she instructed.

Lilly almost opened her mouth to say that she had already given her a cup but stopped herself just in time. 'Yes, I'll take this now,' she said.

She felt a wash of damp cold air in the hallway. The staircase squeaked and groaned all the way up to the landing, where she pushed open the door to her mother's room and went inside. Razor-like shivers ran down her spine and she felt an icy draught on her legs from the crack in the windowsill. The curtains billowed gently into the room, enabling more shadows to dance the walls. Placing the tea and biscuits on the side table, she rubbed her arms.

'It is so cold in here, Mum,' she said. 'You can't be warm enough.'

As she stretched a crocheted blanket under her mother's chin, she noticed the absence of breath. 'Mum, Mum!' she pleaded, but her mother was unresponsive, her face waxy white. Drool had left a slug-like trail down the side of her open mouth.

Lilly knew she had gone. Taking her mother's cold hand, she hugged it against her cheek; it felt heavier now that it was devoid of life. This old bone, skin and flesh had once been her mother. She had passed over with her cloudy white eyes open, as though gazing through the grey fog and watching the shadows entertain her.

Lilly walked calmly to the top of the stairs and tried to compose herself. When she went downstairs, her sister was making sandwiches in the kitchen.

'Here,' Agnes held out a plate, 'take her this. I've just got that ham fresh from the shop. I was lucky to get it as that was the last bit. It will be a lovely treat for her. She hasn't been sick again, has she?'

Lilly managed only a half-whisper, 'Agnes, she's gone.'

Agnes didn't seem to hear her; she was still holding out the plate. 'What was that?'

'She's gone… It's Mother, she's gone.' Lilly tried to raise her voice.

Agnes snapped, 'What do you mean, she's gone? Gone where?' She glared, waiting for an answer.

'She's dead,' Lilly replied, the painful words ringing out into the cold kitchen.

Agnes looked stunned. Her arm descended and she placed the plate back on the table. Time stood still – then her sudden reaction took Lilly by surprise. She had never seen her sister move so fast.

Agnes thundered up the staircase to her mother's bedroom. Suddenly a demonic wail crashed into the silence above. 'No, no, Mummy, no!' she yelled. Then came the uncontrollable sobs and pleading to God. 'Why, why?' she shouted.

After a few seconds her voice fell silent, as if someone had switched off a radio.

Agnes suddenly appeared in the kitchen doorway looking distraught as she struggled her fat arms into her damp raincoat. Her voice was flat. 'I'm going to the phone box to ring the doctor,' she said. Then she was gone, slamming the door hard behind her.

But Lilly could not help noticing that when Agnes had come back into the kitchen, her eyes were bone dry, devoid of any tears.

***

It was a cheap funeral with a black coffin and no flowers. Agnes said they didn't need to waste any more money; their mother wouldn't notice, not now she was dead. She veiled her own face with black lace; Lilly thought maybe it was not to disguise her tears of devastation, but the lack of them.

Lilly's face was open to the elements on that cold misty day as they stood at the graveside watching the black box being lowered into the damp earth. She was proud of her tears; every single one represented the love she'd had for her mother.

Agnes had already started throwing her weight around, donating their mother's threadbare clothes and scuffed shoes to the parish jumble sale. Lilly didn't know if she had found the deeds yet; maybe she had, but she hadn't said anything.

The heavens opened and rain pelted the coffin lid as it waited to be locked away forever in the ground. Mounds of claggy earth surrounded the hole; they hadn't had one dry day in the whole month, and that had made Agnes's moods even more unpredictable. They had been forced by the persistent downpours to stay inside the cottage, and the two sisters with their contrasting personalities clashed constantly. Now that Mother was gone, Lilly wondered who her sister might blame for her outbursts.

Once back at the cottage, they peeled off their heavy coats in the hallway, hung them on a makeshift coat hook made from rusty nails and left them to dry out. It was a little warmer inside the front parlour, but the damp odour didn't give good company.

Lilly watched as Agnes raked out the grate in the chimney breast and tried to get a fire going. The tinder was damp, so when the paper underneath flared the flames didn't take hold. Instead, it sweated and the wood brought forth no warmth, only smoky spirals of stench to intensify the cold dampness in the room.

'I will try again in a while,' said Agnes, sitting next to her sister.

Lilly didn't speak, but acknowledged her with her eyes and a slight nod. Then she stood up. 'I'll make us some tea and bread.'

She went into the kitchen. Absentmindedly, she again thought that her mother was still upstairs and nearly turned to go up to see her. How silly of her. She put the kettle on the stove to boil, then made a pot with three teaspoons of loose tea from a silver tea caddy. Whilst leaving it to brew, she quietly climbed the staircase and entered her mother's room. It looked much the same as always; the only difference was the bed. All the sheets and pillows had been removed, and the naked mattress reinforced the fact that Mother now lay dead in her grave.

Plunging her hand into the bottom drawer of the dresser, she felt under the linen for the large envelope. Pulling the drawer wider, she looked under the sheets where she had left it. There was nothing there.

'Are these what you are looking for?' Her sister was standing in the doorway, her big frame taking up most of the space. Her eyes were glaring, her lips smirking. She was waving the envelope, as though teasing Lilly, slapping the rolled-up document rhythmically into her other hand like a policeman's truncheon. Was Agnes going to attack her with it?

'Oh, Agnes,' Lilly said, putting her hand on her chest, 'you made me jump. I see you already have the deeds that Mother left for us – to share equally.' Her voice was slightly hesitant.

'Equally? What the hell are you talking about?' said Agnes. 'This house is now mine.' Her tone was sharp and her glare full

133

of hatred. 'Don't you know anything, Lilly dear? I am the eldest, I am the next of kin, and this house is now mine!' As she spoke, she grinned with spiteful pleasure, just like the cat who got the cream.

'No Agnes,' protested Lilly. 'That is not what mother wanted, she…'

Before she could finish her sentence, Agnes spat, 'What do you know about what Mother wanted? She told me, yes, *me*, over and over again that I would inherit this cottage.' She was lying, an angry sweat now glossing her skin. 'Just deal with it, little sister. You will never win over me.'

'I don't want to win anything – this isn't a fight. Mother wanted us to share the cottage equally,' Lilly pleaded.

Agnes fell silent for a few seconds, her eyes searching for a way to close the subject. 'Well then,' she demanded, 'prove it!' Turning her back, she marched triumphantly downstairs, leaving her words to fade into the unkind atmosphere.

Lilly knelt over the bottom drawer, flushed with shock and despair. She could hear Agnes in the kitchen below, stirring the teapot, the noise of the spoon clanging up the stairs.

Mother had wanted them to share the house. Feeling alone and wretched, Lilly didn't heed the tears that cascaded down her face.

***

That day, Lilly didn't go downstairs again. She took her mother's crochet blanket into her own bedroom and wrapped it around herself for comfort, praying for some respite from the hollow isolation she felt, and for clarity. What was she to do now?

When evening fell, she heard Agnes skulking outside her bedroom. The floorboards creaked on the landing and her presence cast shadows under her door. Why couldn't they just speak and sort things out sensibly?

Lilly could not go downstairs because her sister now revolted her. She thought her sneaky and cruel; the mere thought of Agnes made her stomach roll with nausea. She felt the terrifying loneliness of her circumstances. Now their mother was gone, how could she possibly live with her spiteful bully of a sister?

She listened to the relentless rain outside as it crashed down on the village of Whalley Dell. A razor-blade flash in the sky speared vibrant white light through her open window, animating prancing shadows and spectral forms against the walls.

Had she anything to live for? Surely death would be a welcome respite from the hell she now found herself in? She resented feeling such a powerful hatred for her older sister; she had never wanted to entertain such feelings for anyone, and she felt guilty about it. It reinforced a cruel self-loathing she had always harboured within her soul. She prayed. *Please God, if you are there, give me strength.*

A rumbling crescendo of thunder rattled the sky, making her feel that her world was tumbling down. She prayed to be back with her mother, prayed for death to take her.

***

The next morning, she awoke to eerie silence. The rain had stopped and the sunlight played hide and seek with bruised, grey clouds. The clock on the side said a quarter to seven.

Feeling helpless and tired, Lilly went downstairs to find Agnes sitting at the kitchen table with tea and bread. Lilly sensed the horrible atmosphere as soon as she walked into the room and it made her fearful.

They did not speak. Lilly made herself breakfast and sat down opposite her sister. Agnes's wheezy breathing dominated the silence, interspersed with the sound of chewing and the slurping of her tea. She smelt of carbolic soap mixed with stale body odour, as though the soap couldn't quite cleanse away her unique spicy-sour scent.

Lilly wanted to say something about the deeds, hoping Agnes would be sensible about them, but she didn't want to go through that pantomime all over again. Then, surprising herself and realising she had nothing to lose, she said, 'I suppose you expect me to leave now that this is your house.'

Agnes, about to take a gulp of tea, stopped abruptly and placed the cup back on the table. Her puffy, early-morning eyes looked even crazier than usual. 'What are you talking about?' she asked.

'Mother said the house was to be shared equally between us. But if this is your house now, where am I to go?'

'No, not this again,' spat Agnes, slamming her plate onto the table. 'It is mine now and there is nothing you can do about it! I will let you stay here, but it is my house now.

You will have to do the household work, the cleaning and cooking, then I will let you stay here rent free.'

'How evil of you, Agnes! Shame on you. If Mother could hear you, she would turn in her grave.'

Agnes laughed. 'Well, she can't can she? So there is nothing you or she can do about it.'

There was a stony silence until Lilly, retrieving some ammunition, suddenly declared, 'Maybe there is something I *can* do about it!'

Agnes, now with her hackles up, said, 'What do you mean? You can't do anything. This house is mine. I don't want to hear another word on the subject.'

'I will go to Mother's solicitor and tell him you have gone against her wishes and stolen the deeds. I can go this afternoon.'

Agnes stood up, scraping the chair legs against the stone floor. She glared at Lilly. 'Stolen? How dare you say such a thing? I have stolen nothing. Anyway, we've finished with the solicitor now and it is all done and dusted. I'm not giving him any more money just for this, do you hear me!'

She was standing close to Lilly, who could smell her stale breath as she screamed the words into her face. 'You can't go all that way to Clinton Brow on your own. You don't know how to get there – and besides, it would take you hours.'

'I'll get the deeds, Agnes. Where are they? Upstairs?' Lilly climbed the staircase to find them.

Agnes ran after her, wheezing as she scaled the steps. She heard Lilly in her bedroom, moving around, opening drawers and looking under furniture. 'Get out of my room, you cheeky bitch!' she cried, running across the hallway, her heavy frame pounding the floorboards.

Lilly didn't care. She was fighting for her survival and it had spawned a rush of determination. She would not let Agnes get away with this; she now had nothing to lose. She knew things would get violent and she had prepared herself: she had taken the rolling pin upstairs with her for protection, concealed inside her dressing-gown pocket.

Feeling it heavy against her hip, she clasped the top of it. If last week had taught her anything, it was to protect herself.

Agnes ran up behind her and grabbed a fistful of Lilly's hair, yanking her backwards from the cupboard and throwing her onto the floor. Lilly tried to use the rolling pin but she dropped it.

Agnes bent to pick it up, shouting furiously, 'Using this to try and fight me, were you?' She held it in her large hand, ready to use it, but Lilly ran for the staircase.

'No, no,' she screamed.

Agnes, sweat now beading her temples, grabbed Lilly again and pulled out chunks of her hair. As it ripped from her bloodied scalp, Lilly felt herself falling forward down the stairs.

Then Agnes was running again, but suddenly her heavy body fell too, squashing Lilly against the wall. Agnes tumbled past her, landing in a mountainous heap at the bottom. The bottom step splintered under her weight.

Silence descended. Lilly could hear her own laboured breath but nothing else. Agnes was motionless and Lilly couldn't see her face. Pain pierced her hand and she looked at it with horror; her fingers were swelling and one of her finger bones had pierced her skin, protruding like a tiny spear of blood-encased ivory.

Lilly tried to get down the staircase but pain shot through her; she realised she must have sprained her ankle. Nobody would find her if she didn't get outside, so she used her elbows and back to steady herself as she eased past Agnes.

Her sister's frantic, bulging eyes were wide open but glassy and motionless. No sound came from her gaping mouth and Lilly knew she was dead. She needed to get help!

Fuelled by adrenalin, she pulled herself over her sister's fat carcass and dragged herself to the door. She opened it. *Phone box, I need to get to the phone box,* she thought.

Just then a voice shouted her name through the noisy wind. 'Lilly, Lilly is that you? What has happened – are you okay?' She turned to see her neighbour, Gladys, approaching.

137

'Oh, thank God,' panted Lilly. 'It's my sister Agnes – she's fallen down the stairs and I think she's dead. It was an accident.'

'Alright, Lilly. Look at your hand – you need the hospital! Go back inside and I will get help.'

'No, no, I can't go back with her lying there!'

Gladys took hold of Lilly's good hand and they walked as fast as they could to the phone box. Squeezing inside, Gladys dialled 999. 'Hello? Police please, and an ambulance. There has been a very bad accident at 6 Meadow Row, Whalley Dell. Please hurry.'

***

Like the ripple of a stone thrown into a pond, the real world came back. Cassandra and Sabina found themselves in the pristine bedroom of the cottage once more…

'Oh my God,' said Cassandra, overwhelmed, as they looked at one another.

'That certainly explains why she won't let go of this place,' said Sabina.

'What can we do? How can I get her to go?'

'She may have already gone.'

'You mean that was it – she's gone now?' Cassandra asked.

'Maybe. But we need to make sure with a prayer to move her on to the other side. We need the help of our guides in spirit to open a portal of light, and we need to light a white candle.'

Cassandra went downstairs to get the candle and matches from the kitchen drawer, then ran back up. The room was calm, with no indication of ghostly interference, yet they could feel pockets of coldness here and there. She lit the candle, allowing its flame to swell and elongate from its wick, its golden glow softening the atmosphere.

She and Sabina held hands as Sabina prayed to the spirit of love and light to take the soul of Agnes for redemption in heaven. Filling the room with positivity, they waited until they felt a swirl of angelic energy spin gently from the ceiling. As it descended, the room was glazed with bright white-and-golden light. There was an overwhelming sense of benevolence as a tunnel opened up before them.

'Please Agnes, go to the light. You have no fear of punishment. Let the light take you home,' said Sabina.

They heard a screeching protest; it seemed far away, a hollow communication from another world. Sabina repeated, 'Go to the light, Agnes. Don't be afraid. They will help you to heal and move on to your next life. Let them take you.'

She and Cassandra allowed a higher intelligence to take over, and a sense of peace and love stretched hungrily into the room. Then they saw Agnes, her frightened eyes and hesitant stance hunched over in the corner of the room.

Asserting herself, Cassandra shouted, 'Let them take you, Agnes. Let them…'

In a split- second Agnes and the light were gone, swallowed up by a higher dimension. A happy silence descended upon the house, replacing her spirit.

Looking at one another in triumph, Sabina and Cassandra sat on the bed and basked in the new atmosphere. 'Well done, Cassandra,' Sabina said. 'That's your second spirit release. How do you feel?'

Cassandra started to laugh; it had given her a new perspective on existence and she was no longer afraid. A new chapter in her life was starting, and it was endowing her with a new confidence.

***

After Sabina left, Cassandra breezed into the kitchen. Making tea and toast, she felt chirpy and the new vibrations imbued her with a powerful sense of protection and a reassurance that everything would be alright. Joyfully, she prepared for the evening ahead. There was more reason to celebrate now than just moving in; she had banished the spectre, sending it on its way not with cruel vengeance but with love and light. A win-win all round, and that was what she liked.

139

33

Saffron paced through the lush meadow towards the caravan, intending to drop by and see Cassandra. She didn't know that Cassandra had already moved into her cottage. Climbing the wooden steps, she tried the door. It was locked, and the windows were not only closed but shuttered. Had her spell worked so soon?

Saffron prowled around the abandoned dwelling, looking for signs of life, then looked towards the wood. A hazy figure of a man stood by its entrance. Unmoving, he seemed to be staring at her.

She marched forward confidently, not intimidated but curious to know who he was. As she approached, he slowly turned away and disappeared into the trees.

Entering behind him, Saffron's vision gradually adjusted and she scanned all around to see where he'd gone. Walking cautiously along the path next to the stream, she realised he was not there yet she continued.

She noticed some small white flowers ahead and decided to harvest some, knowing they had a sumptuous fragrance. Then, feeling a rush of frustration, she started to shred their perfect petals and rip them apart with her claw-like fingernails. All the while, she was thinking of Cassandra and the revulsion she felt for her stealing Fenton.

It was like a potent spell; a sweet, ripe aroma released into the air and tickled her nose. She breathed it in. She felt a shift in the atmosphere behind her and turned to see a handsome young man staring at her with an impish smile on his face. His hair was short and blond, his skin flawlessly shaven except for an almost invisible goatee beard, and his eyes were pale blue.

He smiled at her and his eyes seemed to look into her soul. Shocked at his sudden presence and close proximity, Saffron instinctively stepped backwards.

'Not having a good day, Saffron?' he asked. His gaze fell onto the torn petals.

'Who are you? How do you know my name?' she asked.

'Oh, I've seen you coming and going in these woods for a while now. Let me introduce myself. My name is Ruben … Ruben Capricornus.' He bowed slowly, waving his arm as if in the company of royalty. He didn't seem to be dressed for this century but was wearing woollen trousers and a linen smock. A crystal the colour of his eyes dangled from his neck on a long silver chain. Sunlight from it disturbed her vision, and she was sure the pupils of his eyes suddenly changed from circular to horizontal slits – not unlike those of a goat. But how could that be?

Although not very broad in stature, he held an invisible power, and his charm and demeanour hypnotised her into a false sense of security. He was too smooth, too charming, too perfect.

'I'm here to help you, Saffron. I know you are troubled and things are not happening as they should. Here, drink this herbal wine and it will bring you comfort.' He held out a bottle of white wine with a faded label on it.

Dazed, and in awe of his gift to her, she lifted it from his hands and tried to read the medieval script. 'Vesper stella?' she asked.

He produced two small silver drinking vessels and handed one to her. Retrieving the bottle, he twisted his hand and the cork popped the air. 'Let us sit a while and talk and get to know each other,' he said, pouring the clear liquid into her cup. It tasted of sweet honey and lemon but with a refreshing twist when she swallowed.

Feeling the liquid trickle down her throat, Saffron felt a sudden rush of euphoria. Looking down, she noticed he had placed a silk blanket on the ground. It was ornately stitched with a tapestry of colourful flowers and greenery. He knelt upon it and held out his arm for her to join him.

She surrendered to his powerful charm and his seduction began, gently at first then more intense. Rapture and more rapture: they were melting into a swirling vortex of passion that she didn't want to end.

34

Cassandra allowed the warmth of the afternoon to trespass from the top half of the stable door in the kitchen. It seemed to cleanse away any tensions and lift the mood in the house to one of peace and tranquillity. The music from the radio teased her mood with excitement.

A selection of sandwiches, small cheese pies and sausage rolls decorated her table, displaying her attempt at entertaining her guests. Nothing too formal; after all, it was only Sabina, Charity – and Fenton, of course. Her guests would feel welcome without feeling any tension that she'd gone to too much trouble. It would be a happy relaxed affair.

Time was progressing. At 5.10pm, she decided to ready herself for the evening ahead. Inside her beautiful bathroom, she switched on the shower. Stepping beneath it, into the firm blast of water, it cascaded over her skin. The noise of the shower drowned out the music from the radio downstairs.

Rinsing away the tensions of the day, she felt energised. She wondered what to wear for the evening and she toyed with a few options. Stepping across the landing in her robe, she felt a blast of coolness as she crossed the threshold of her bedroom.

The room felt mellow; a welcoming breeze was teasing through the open window. As she dressed, Cassandra's attention was suddenly alerted to noises downstairs in the kitchen It was the sound of someone rummaging. Had an intruder sneaked into the house? She had left the stable door open and anyone could have entered without her knowledge.

'Hello, who's there?' she shouted down the twisting staircase from the top landing.

Running downstairs into the kitchen, she was met by nothing but gentle music from the radio pulsating through an eerie emptiness. Everything was as she had left it. Looking around the rooms she satisfied herself that nobody had sneaked in, then closed and locked the back door.

She continued to get ready. Finding her favourite aqua-blue and chocolate-brown silk dress, she put on some makeup and teased at her short strands of hair. She admired her sun-kissed reflection in the full-length mirror: she looked and felt fantastic.

Downstairs, the setting sunshine had moved away from the kitchen window. Someone was standing outside the kitchen window looking in; a man was staring at her. He was young, blond and handsome with strange eyes. As she approached the window, he waved then melted away into nothing. *How strange.*

The vision was only fleeting and, unmoved after everything else she had witnessed in Whalley Dell, Cassandra turned up the volume on the radio.

There was a knock on the door; it was Fenton and he was early. He was carrying a bottle of champagne and a bunch of red roses. She kissed him on the cheek, her full warm lips feeling his clean, smoothly shaven skin. She let them linger against his face for a long time, then laughed. 'You're early but I don't mind at all,' she said.

'Is anyone here yet, or am I the first?'

'You are the first.'

'Oh, baby, come here.' He pulled her towards him and placed his hungry lips upon hers, kissing her until she could hardly breathe. He took her hands and they embraced and kissed and talked until Sabina and Charity arrived half an hour later.

Flush-faced, Cassandra let them in, adjusting her dress as she went to open the door.

Sabina and Charity didn't stay long – they wanted to give Cassandra and Fenton some space. And after they left, the night heated up into one of passionate lovemaking and soulful rapture.

35

When Saffron awoke, Ruben Capricornus was gone but the ornate blanket and empty bottle of wine remained. Evening was approaching and the noise in the branches and the undergrowth seemed to intensify as the sun plunged into the horizon. A wavy undulating darkness crept in around her.

Not quite remembering what had taken place, she stood on the blanket and looked around. She could hardly focus. Her hair felt dishevelled and her dress stretched and creased.

She was trying to remember what had happened when she noticed a cold chill had descended. A shadowy presence was up ahead and, as she approached cautiously, Saffron realised it was the hag, her pipe jutting from her mouth, her skeletal fingers wrapped around it. Those vibrant blue eyes were the only colour piercing through her sooty grey form.

'Ye had to do it, didn't ye?' said the hag. 'Ye danced with the devil and there is no going back now. He has you in his grip.' Rusty teeth moved as she spoke.

Saffron was puzzled. 'What do you mean? I don't remember anything…' Her eyes searched the wilderness for a memory.

The hag gave a wry smile. 'What ye put out, ye will get back. Your jealousy and anger summoned him into this world. Ye should have let the fates have their way – ye cannot change the fates lest ye dance with the devil, lass. Ye tried to poison that girl, and ye did witchcraft with dolls.' Cackling, she added, 'A banishment spell is tame, but you had murderous intent. You have summoned evil and trickery into the world, you silly girl. It has come back to ye full circle. You're on your own now, I can do nothing for ye.'

Then she was gone. Saffron turned around to look at the colourful blanket under the tree and suddenly remembered what had taken place upon it. Shock engulfed her. On the blanket, she saw someone who looked familiar: it was her own remains and she had been violated. The devil had done his dirty deed.

She tried to stretch out her arm in front of her but could see no hands. She was invisible. She ran to the stream and peered into a pool of clear water – but she could not see her own reflection. She was no longer of this world, and her dead body lay in a mutilated heap on the blanket. Then Ruben Capricornus appeared from the dank shadows. She begged him for mercy, but her futile cries were ignored. She followed behind him, as he dragged her into the deep, knotted terrain. A vortex tunnel opened up and swallowed her marred corpse into its gluttonous orifice, to rot into an earthen soup. Her remains would never be found - Her fate, to witness the blissful life Cassandra and Fenton would have together … and to dwell in Dead Man's Wood forever.

Printed in Great Britain
by Amazon

19021704R00088